Big Rock

Passion in the Pacific

Reggie Brick

CONTENT WARNING: The main character in this book battled with temporary anorexia. She experienced it in her quest to complete a challenging athletic event. The hero in this book struggled with PTSD and had a flash back memory of a traumatic event in his job. If this may be triggering for you, please put your mental health first and proceed with caution or skip this story completely.

eBook Edition ISBN-979-8-9902179-0-4:

Paperback ISBN-979-8-9902179-1-1

Cover design by GetCovers

Contents

Dedicated to...
My patient, generous, and loving husband;
and to
My inspirational daughters.

Publishing with a Purpose

Nursing Scholarship and Lahaina Support

The town of Lahaina, Maui is a special place for my family and me. The devastation of the fire on August 8, 2023 caused heartbreaking death and destruction for residents there. I will donate 5% of my net proceeds from this book to Lahaina organizations that support Lahaina locals.

Nurses are the reason for this series because they are amazing angels on earth. Nursing has been a tradition of strong women in my family and I pledge that five percent of my net proceeds will be placed in a scholarship fund for nursing students. Funds will be distributed annually. Please fill out a form for your nominations for this scholarship at
https://linktr.ee/reggiebrick

Chapter 1

Fantasy Island

A leggy brunette navigated the unfamiliar, narrow streets of Honolulu on her twelve-speed bike en route to Queen's Hospital. A refreshing morning mist gently kissed her face and neck while she pedaled closer to a vibrant rainbow crowning the mountain ahead. Tiny drops from above mixed with beads of sweat on her skin and created a sensation of pure refreshment. Humid breezes from morning trade winds and a whooshing motion on her bike made her feel energized and serene.

"Jeez-us! Back off, brah!" Jenae screamed at a rolling metal behemoth as she squeezed both handlebar breaks and jolted to a stop.

The bus driver tried to scare her off by running her off the road into the gutter. His disapproving side eye, cheeky smirk, and a puff of black diesel exhaust gave her second thoughts about taking that route to work, but it wouldn't deter the excitement of her first official day of work as a traveling nurse.

Jenae donned a royal blue fanny pack that was stuffed with a pair of green hospital scrubs, a comb, deodorant, a stethoscope, beef jerky, and cash. She was contracted to work shifts at the hospital, but she was mostly eager to conquer the island of Oahu during her off time. Jenae was young and fit and couldn't believe her luck to work in paradise with two friends who transmuted with her from Texas. Although she and her best girlfriends worked at different hospitals, Jenae expected they'd strengthen their bonds and be tanned beach buddies for the summer. In her perfect fantasy, she'd find a beautiful, strong, kind man to take back with her to Texas. Jenae was often in her own head, pondering if she could find her husband by the end of the summer.

Something in her heart told her she would.

Jenae started to cool down as she parked her bike in a shady spot at the entrance of the hospital. She spotted a bike rack situated on the side of the building between clusters of palm trees. As she locked her bike with a cable loop, she heard mewing from a nearby hedge. A scrawny yellow mama cat with long teats slowly sauntered through the canopy.

"Aw, poor lady." Jenae squatted down in the shade next to her to get a closer look. She was careful not to touch the feral cat, and through the hedge, she could see five baby kittens in a pile lying on top of each other. As they squirmed and stretched, Jenae could see that they had different coat colors, and their eyes were already open. "Here, mama, have some of my beef jerky." Jenae had rustled through her fanny pack, broke off pieces of the dehydrated meat and threw them into the cat's path. She poured cold water from her water bottle into a plastic cup that she found next to a trashcan and left it near the kitten den for when the mama cat decided to return to her duties.

Jenae dashed into the side entrance of the hospital, worried that she would be late for her first shift. She quickly freshened up with a splash of water around her neck and underarms, applied a wipe of deodorant on each armpit, and changed into scrubs in the public bathroom. Jenae took in two quick breaths and one big exhale. The familiar and distinct smell of hospital disinfectant she knew so well from hospitals in Texas gave her a sense of confidence. Her running shoes screeched and squeaked on the newly polished linoleum floors as she walked to the 1 Mauka post–op surgical floor. She heard the early news broadcast blaring on a TV from the waiting room; President Ronald Reagan was talking about an Iran-Contra scandal.

The charge nurse with dyed black hair amid silver roots greeted her with a stern Hawaiian Filipino accent.

"Aloha, are you Jenae, our new traveler? Don't forget to clock in on the computer. Did you take the bus to work? How long are you here for?"

"Hi, yes, it's very nice to meet you." Jenae shook her hand with composure even though the barrage of questions made her dizzy.

"I'm here for three months this summer, and I rode my bike to the hospital from Waikiki. Thanks for giving me the opportunity," Jenae said. *Three months is going to fly by fast... maybe I should stay longer.*

The middle-aged manager was all business with her firing-squad questions.

"You rode a bike? Why do you have a bike? Most people take the bus," she said as she turned around and walked away down the hallway, not expecting an answer.

The word *haoli* (white girl who doesn't belong here) wasn't uttered out loud, but Jenae could read her superior's opinions as if a thought bubble floated above her head. The wise nurse manager had dealt with mainland nurses before and knew their true intentions for coming to Hawaii. Jenae didn't even try to assuage her skepticism: *Who comes to Hawaii to build their nursing skills?* She had more than enough experience and education to power through this three-month gig with one hand tied behind her back... or so she thought.

Jenae jumped right in to meet her co-workers and rounded on her patients after the morning shift report. Orientation in HR with the other newbies for the past few days was the easy part. Shortly after assessing her assigned patients, two more back-to-back post-ops returned to the floor after surgery more quickly than Jenae had anticipated.

Patient 1 had a broken bone reset in his arm after his scooter hit a patch of sand on the roadway. He was a tourist from the mainland. *Note to self,* Jenae thought, *do not rent scooters, and definitely make friends with bus drivers.*

Patient 2 was another young man who underwent a surgical extraction of a foreign object from his rectum. He was a local resident and had family members waiting for him in his patient room when he returned from post-op recovery. It was more awkward for Jenae than for them. A vibrator had moved up into his sigmoid colon when the juddering created a suction that was impossible to release without doing more damage. Jenae held her smirk, scanning the room with bulged eyeballs as she mentally recalled a bad joke a surgical resident once told her in San Antonio...*Hey Doc, thanks for removing my vibrator toy from down there. Doc checks the chart, adjusts his reading glasses, rechecks the chart, and replies, "Sorry, I thought you just wanted me to change the batteries."*

―――――◆○◆―――――

The traveling nurse position was handed to Jenae on a silver platter after a hiring agent called to interview her on the phone. Jenae's friends, Hannah and Pami, from San Antonio, had offered up her name to the agency because they wanted to have one last hurrah before Jenae started her Master's in Business Administration degree in Dallas that fall. She was employed at a medical center in Dallas at the time, where she really enjoyed working with a cohesive staff; her nurse manager was a good friend, too.

Jenae couldn't decide for weeks if she would join her friends in Hawaii that summer. Her reluctance was fueled by anxiety over finding a spot for her dog to stay and the upcoming transition to business school. After long talks with her mom and boss, Jenae decided to take the leap and fly to Honolulu with her friends for a summer of fun. They'd convinced her that the timing to take a sabbatical was perfect; Jenae's lease had expired, and her mom agreed to take care of her dog, Gremlin, for the summer. She'd be back in the fall to start her MBA, and her boss promised that she would be rehired and could pick up weekend shifts at the medical center when she returned.

Once the decision to spend a summer in the Pacific settled in, Jenae daydreamed about what life would be like in the sunny tropics. Getting away for a while would be a good way to gain perspective on her entire life and formulate her wishes for the future.

She'd just broken up with a great guy with a premiere education who sold commercial real estate in L.A. He'd alluded to marriage a few times, and at a romantic setting on the Santa Monica Pier, he grabbed her hands, smiled adoringly, and said, "I love you, Jenae." She couldn't say it back. The weekend was a bust, and the relationship was broken. He couldn't handle the rejection and quickly called the whole thing off. Perhaps true love would never be forthcoming for her because she'd failed at so many promising relationships.

Many of Jenae's friends had married out of high school or shortly after college graduation; some of them had two children already. The pull to be a mother had always tugged on her heart, and it got stronger as time ticked by. The balance of career and settling down was a constant struggle. She had personal, educational, and career goals but didn't think she could achieve them with the responsibilities of marriage and motherhood. She often thought to herself - *Would a serious relationship get in the way? Am I really ready to settle down? Maybe my competitiveness pushes guys away.*

Most loudly, her mother's voice entered her head, and her knees would go weak. *"What do you do to drive them away, Jenae? You must be doing something."*

Jenae tried to keep an optimistic attitude on the surface to veil her insecurities that made her feel unworthy of true love.

Maybe I'm not worthy of finding a crushing love in this lifetime.

I want the kind of love that gives me continuous flutters in my heart and tummy when I think of him.

I want to feel warm and secure, like I'm home in his arms.

I want the kind of love where I can see far into the future - when I have gray hair, he has creaky bones, and we chase our grandchildren around the garden.

She knew full well that her heart could be broken again, but naive resilience kept Jenae's heart open to romance and adventure in paradise.

Chapter 2

Adulting in San Antonio

Jenae started her very first nursing job at age twenty-two, immediately after graduation from a university in the middle of a wheat field. Moving to San Antonio involved a long relocation drive south on Interstate 35 in a lemon yellow VW Beetle with her older sister-sitting shotgun. After securing an apartment in San Antonio and checking in with the hospital HR lady to sign paperwork, they drove to the Gulf of Mexico. During a gas station stop, they picked up some highly processed snacks, diet sodas, and big brown bottles of cheap beer. Their plan included spending the night parked on the beach, crunched up in the front seats of the VW with a blanket and pillow each. Instead of sleeping, they talked, laughed, and complained about almost everything. In a game of "truth or dare," the dare usually involved doing a gymnastic maneuver on the hard sand or running topless into the surf. When unwanted attention from young scruffy men approached, they screamed, giggled, and sped off in the backfiring VW to a safer location down the beach. As the sun rose and the moon set, the sisters managed to grab a catnap before hitting the road north, back to San Antonio.

———◦◦◦———

At the medical center in San Antonio, Jenae worked with a delightful best friend on an adult surgical floor but often found herself getting reprimanded by the charge nurse for not catching on quickly enough as a graduate nurse. Charge nurse Barbie tried to live up to her name; she'd perfected a dolled-up manager look, which included a light blonde fur coat over her tight white nursing uniform with pink ribbons in her hair. Barbie frequently went off campus for two-hour dinners with her middle-aged boyfriend and left Jenae to cover an extended patient load. "Jenae, make sure you give my surgical patient two full bags of enema fluid while I'm gone. His surgery is first thing in the morning, and his doctor will be upset if he isn't shining like a rosebud." *I wonder if Barbie knows that we really call her Cruella de Vil?*

Later that summer, after Jenae passed her Texas licensing boards and became a full-fledged Registered Nurse, she applied to Labor and Delivery and NICU because she had met Pami and a few other nurses in the cafeteria who encouraged her to fill an opening on their unit. She seemed to jive with them better and loved working with babies, but she didn't realize that she'd have to change a few of her ways to fit in.

When Jenae transferred to the NICU, she didn't have many vices, not even drinking coffee in the morning. She quickly fell to peer pressure and took up a cigarette habit because there was only one break room on the unit, and almost every nurse there pulled and puffed on Marlboro cowboy killers and Menthol Lights on their dinner breaks. Jenae tried to resist initially but figured she'd smoked the occasional ciggy while out at the clubs and was inhaling secondhand smoke in the blue and white haze without the buzz, anyway. "Hey, can I bum a cigarette from you? Anyone got a light?" Jenae asked. She felt the bond tighten with her fellow nightingales as they happily welcomed her into their nicotine club. It was a connection that fostered a robust social life both on the unit during work and at local dive bars in south Texas after they finished their shifts at eleven.

Evening shift work was a natural fit for young RNs without husbands or children or early morning obligations. Workmates Pami, Hannah, Jenae, and Mel met up a couple of nights a week to close down the bar across the main road from the hospital. "A long-neck bottle of Corona with two limes, please." Jenae ordered from the waitress. The rhythm of reggae music and outdoor tables with sand under their feet was a perfect place to wind down after their shift. They felt like they were on a beach in South Padre Island.

Nobody but fellow nurses knew the real technical and emotional work that went into the job. Attachments that formed between nurses weren't unlike soldiers' battlefield bonds. Long debriefs over a few beers were often the best medicine to ward off PTSD, but sometimes a ten-minute cry in the car all by oneself in the parking lot could release a lot of stress, too. Working with the same group of nurses for two years created a tight-knit group.

"Ah, I love the warm summer breeze blowing down my neck and the cool sand between my toes. But, I haven't seen any cute boys here yet," Jenae said.

"Is that the only thing that matters to you, Jenae, finding a husband?" Mel responded.

"It's high up there on my to-do list, Mel. But I don't want to find just anyone; I want to find the right husband. One who'll write me love notes every day and promise to be with me for eternity. Besides, we're well into the marriage age bracket, and some say we're old maids already. You're the one with the cat, Mel."

Mel threw her head back and then forward with her chin on her chest while giving Jenae an - *are you serious?* Stare.

Jenae's sister just got engaged and was planning her wedding, and Jenae took it as a sign to start looking for Mr. Right. She'd dated several men and even lived with a Brit against her better judgment. She felt she should do the right thing when his doctor convinced Jenae that she needed to take care of him after a major surgery. She'd saved herself for intimate relations until she was twenty-two but gave up her virginity to someone she liked a lot but didn't love. Jenae pined for a true romantic love that hadn't yet materialized. "I only seem to attract needy guys who want to latch on for dear life or a guy with a few months left on his student visa." Jenae gravitated toward exotic, international men to extract herself from her mundane, Mid-western upbringing.

"Amen to that sister. Let's find some real men," Hannah said. Hannah was very experienced with boys, starting in high school. It was also the same time her dad left her mom and the family for a younger woman. She felt comfortable flirting with guys that she liked because she knew she could get what she wanted by putting out sexually. It was fun for her and very fruitful for her dating record. Hannah was comfortable having casual sex with guys to garner attention.

"Oh hey, there's a table of guys over there; never mind, they look too young, and that one guy has a creepy mustache, ew," Hannah said.

"Well, the cutest one is coming over, and he's mine, ladies. I already winked at him." Pami grinned and batted her big brown eyes. Pami was an experienced temptress, like Hannah. She had many handsome boyfriends and some could be considered out of her league. There was something about Pami, which kept them around.

"Ugh, I'm glad I didn't bother to change out of my scrubs tonight," Mel said as she rolled her eyes, knowing that she was last in line to find a guy. Mel had always been single and despised the beaus of her friends. Her father was a Major League Baseball player in his day but became an abusive husband and father when his career washed up.

Pami and Jenae often staffed the receiving room for newly born babies together. "Who wants to be charge nurse today?" Pami said at the start of a shift in the admissions nursery. Jenae knew she'd have to do it since there were just the two of them there. "We have four deliveries coming on our shift so far: There are three full-term but one with meconium staining, and one preemie. Who's feeling lucky starting IV's today? I drank too much last night, so Jenae, you're it." Pami turned up the radio to a perky tune and sang along. *Wake me up before you go, go.* Jenae joined in as she snapped her fingers with George Michael's signature moves. "OK, I'll be charge nurse for you today, but you owe me one," Jenae said.

Spending the shifts with good friends made work at the hospital something to look forward to. Pami and Jenae had each other's backs, whether it was covering vacations at work, helping to move, or being good wing women.

Charge nurse meant placing teeny tiny IVs into teeny tiny veins in newborns' scalps when they needed antibiotics. It also meant starting the first feeding with mom and baby, as well as diplomatically communicating with enthusiastic grandmas. Pami and Jenae taught pre-birth parenting classes once a week in the evenings, which allowed them to form relationships with the parents prenatally.

Jenae told Pami, "It's kind of weird that neither of us has had a baby, but we are telling parents what to do."

"Your mom is the breastfeeding guru, so it must be in your blood," Pami said.

"I suppose, my whole childhood, I watched moms and babies come to our house for monthly La Leche League meetings. Maybe I'll be in one of her breastfeeding textbooks with my baby one day."

"Well, you have the boobs for it. My baby might starve to death, and I wouldn't make pictorials with my top off."

"We know that isn't how it works. I'm sure your future babies will have plenty of milk. My favorite part of being charge nurse, by far, is congratulating the moms from our class (including the flat chested ones) and helping the baby latch on for their first feeding."

Chapter 3

Landing on Big Rock

Plane reservations to Honolulu were scheduled for Hannah and Jenae together through Los Angeles by the nurse's travel agency. Jenae still had doubts about gallivanting off to Hawaii for the summer, but there was no turning back now that her furniture was in a storage unit and Gremlin was safely hanging out with Grandma.

"I love the double-decker 747 plane. It makes me feel like I'm in a nightclub flying over the Pacific Ocean. Do you think I could sneak up to the top floor?" Hannah looked up the spiral staircase while she leaned against the semi-circle bar at the front of the plane. "There are some guys I met in the gate area who are seated up there. They said that they live on the North Shore, and they invited us to a beach party next week." "Well, that was fast," Jenae replied. Hannah was short, blonde, and wore her hair in a high sideways ponytail. Hannah's demeanor and looks resembled Betty Boop, with her big blue eyes and smirky smile. She also had an uncanny knowledge of baseball statistics, which mesmerized most guys she met. Hannah was

17

a first class flirt. Jenae felt like a massive cow next to her. They had a strong friendship because they went everywhere together, even though they were polar opposites: professional basketball games, state fairs, concerts, and now Hawaii.

"Hey, don't let me forget to call Teeim when we land. He's going to pick us up from the airport and take us to our hotel when we get to Honolulu," Hannah said.

"Now, how do you know Tim, exactly?"

"Teeim and I were good friends in Galveston growing up. He played football at the Naval Academy, and now he's stationed at the Marine base here in Kaneohe."

"Sounds promising. We're getting off to a good start." Jenae rested her head against the window in an economy seat at the back of the plane.

The view of Pearl Harbor during the approach to the airport took Jenae to a learned memory in her mind as she imagined the track that the Japanese kamikaze pilots took when they bombed the harbor in 1941. Images of huge splashes where bombs hit and black fuel fires engulfing broken battleships crossed her mind. She remembered a Veteran's Day account of the attack given by her friend's father in elementary school about running from his family's base housing on a Sunday morning to alert others. He told the class that thousands were killed that day.

"Hey! There's Teeim over there in the red pickup truck. Teeim, Teeim!" Hannah yelled, jumping up and down with her arms waving over her head. Tim waved back with the biggest smile and brought the truck closer to the curb at the Honolulu Airport. "Welcome to Hawaii, ladies!" Tim said in a thick Texas accent. "Let me get your luggage." "Thanks for picking us up, Teeim," replied Hannah in her best flirty southern drawl. "The pleasure is all mine. Wow, I get to ride with the two prettiest gals on the island," Tim said with a grin and a twinkle in his eyes. Jenae was smitten from the start. *He's hunky and knows how to flirt too, I bet Hannah has plans to date him this summer, though. Oh well, maybe he has some cute Marine friends that I could meet.* Jenae thought to herself.

"Oh, Teeim, you are such a sweetheart. Do you know where our hotel is? The travel agency said it's in Waikiki. Is that close to your apartment?" Hannah said with a Cheshire smile.

"It's not too far from my place, you'll see. Hey, after you get checked in, do you want to grab some dinner at a Korean place tonight? It's not too far, just around the corner," Tim said.

"That'd be great, but you may have to order for me because I don't think I've ever eaten Korean food. We only have Chinese restaurants in south Texas, remember?" Hannah replied.

"Oh, you will love it. I'll pick you both up at seven. That should give you time to settle in."

"Sounds great. Thanks for the ride, Tim. It was nice to meet you. See you in a bit." Jenae grabbed her bags and set them on the sidewalk.

The girls checked into a nondescript, concrete, middle-budget hotel that was more off an alleyway than the main drag. It had a pool that didn't get any sun because it was in the shade of high rises all around. The girls had two rooms reserved by the travel agency, but they decided to stay together in one double-double room for safety and support. "Yay! We made it to Hawaii, and we don't have to start orientation until Monday morning. We have all weekend to explore and get our bearings," Jenae said gleefully as she jumped backward on her bed in a starfish formation. "I hope Ronin, the cute guy from the plane, calls me. I gave him the name of our hotel," Hannah lamented.

The Korean restaurant was rated one star for price and three stars for food. The atmosphere was 1.5 stars, with fluorescent lighting, laminate tables, and two metal racks at the door holding weekly magazines (some in English, but most in characters from another language).

"I love this marinated grilled chicken," Jenae said.

"Try the kimchi salad and follow it with some rice," Tim said.

"What's kimchi?" Jenae asked.

"It is a Korean salad made with fermented cabbage and a lot of spicy stuff. You'll feel the full effect tomorrow morning when it wakes you up in the bathroom."

"Teeim, you are disgusting. Why would you have us eat such a thing!" Hannah replied.

"Have another beer, that will help." Tim winked at both girls.

After dinner, Tim and the girls walked down the street and passed a generic bar near the Korean joint. It wasn't evident from the lack of signage what was inside, but Tim insisted that they go in for a quick drink. They could feel a bass beat resonate as they walked through the canvas curtain just inside the doorway. Low red lights, smoky air, and a sparse crowd of desperate-looking middle-aged men looking up toward a stage at a figure moving through the haze made it evident that they were in a strip club. Tim bent over, holding his belly, and laughed at the girls' expressions when Hannah and Jenae caught sight of a seasoned, saggy stripper dancing on the pole. The performer's eyes were closed as she swayed side to side of the pole in a G-string, most likely imagining herself somewhere else far, far away. "What the heck?" Jenae punched Tim in the arm. Tim bit his lip, laughed, and quickly whisked them outside and back on the sidewalk stroll to his truck. "What, we aren't staying for a drink, Teeim?" Hannah joked.

At the hotel, the girls showered and prepared for a good night's sleep.

"I can't believe we are going to bed at ten o'clock, but I guess it is 2 AM Central time. I'm exhausted; we've had a long travel day." Jenae turned to the ringing phone on the side table between the beds as Hannah picked up the receiver.

"Howdy! Sure, I remember you, Ronin. I'm glad you found me. Tomorrow? Sure, that sounds like fun! I'll see if my

roommate wants to come, but for sure, pick me up at noon."
Jenae couldn't help but overhear Hannah's conversation on
the phone.

"Hey, that was one of the guys I met from the plane ride
over; he's the hot one who lives on the North Shore. Do you
want to go to a cookout on the beach there tomorrow with
me? He's going to pick us up."

"Oh, no, I don't think so. That's really nice of you to offer,
but I didn't really meet him, and I kind of want to get situated
before training starts on Monday. I will just stay here and run
some errands. Are you OK going by yourself?"

"I'm perfectly fine going by myself, but I don't want to
desert you on our first full day here."

"Don't worry about that. I'm a big girl. Do you need me to
pick anything up from the store for you?"

"No thanks, I think I'm set for a while. But maybe we could
go to the DMV together this week and get our Hawaii driver
licenses. Ronin said that we get can get discounts for rental
cars and activities with a local ID. It's called the Kamaaina rate,
which means friendly or local or something along those lines."

"Oh, cool. Sounds like a plan. Lights out, I'm about to pass
out." Jenae faded quickly into a deep sleep.

Just as he promised, the handsome, built Asian guy from
the plane picked Hannah up at noon from the front of the
hotel. She and Ronin zipped down the Ala Wai in his sporty
Mazda with big, toothy smiles as the wind blew through their
hair. Hannah focused on Ronin's high cheekbones and his

muscular, strong arms. She couldn't wait to see him in his swim trunks when they got to the North Shore. Hannah and Ronin talked about family and friends on their hour-long journey in traffic.

"I'm from Houston originally; that's where I went to nursing school. My mama and daddy still live there. They're split up, but I see them both a lot."

"I spent a week in Houston for training with my firm. It's too bad we never met there," Ronin said.

"I would've remembered you if we'd met. Did you learn commodities training there? We're known for our oil in south Texas. Besides, I might not have been there, anyway. I moved to San Antonio after I graduated to try someplace new. That's where I met my two girlfriends who are here doing traveling nursing with me."

"So you said on the plane that you take care of sick babies?"

"Yep, I love working with babies and young children. I became intrigued with it during my pediatric clinical. We never really got to take care of neonatal ICU patients in nursing school, but it was a challenge that I wanted to pursue."

"Well, that sounds really hard and emotional."

"It's hard in some ways, but I've met some amazing nurses and made really good friends on the unit. Our third friend, Pami, is coming out in a few weeks, and she will be working with me in the ICU at the Children's Hospital. I work in the NICU for newborn babies and Pami will be in the PICU for older pediatric patients."

"So, how many nurses are coming from Texas this summer?"

"Just Me, Pami, and Jenae in our group. Jenae's the girl from the plane and my roommate while we're here. She'll be working at Queen's Hospital on a medical/surgical floor. I heard Queen's is the major trauma center in the state."

"Knock on wood, I've never been a patient in the hospital, but if I ever was, I'd feel better having all of you pretty nurses taking care of me. In any case, it sounds like you gals are going to have a great summer together."

"We've had really fun times when we visited each other for the occasional weekend in Houston, Dallas, or San Antonio. It's been hard not being able to hang out much this past year, which is why we are going to do it this summer in Hawaii."

"Why didn't Jenae want to come with us today? My roommates are always looking for a cute date."

"She's getting things ready for training next week, and I think she needs time to acclimate and figure out how to get around."

"Maybe next time."

"Besides, she's kind of stuffy and can be a real Debbie Downer when she's stressed out. I can bring her to the North Shore on another weekend when she's more settled in."

Hannah and Ronin stopped by the liquor store for a case of beer and a bag of chips.

"Yum, I can't wait to try those Maui chips." Hannah opened the bag of chips with a pop. "Do you commute to

Honolulu every morning from the North Shore? This seems like a long drive for a little island."

"My firm is in Honolulu, and as a commodities trader, I have to drive over in the middle of the night because trading starts on East Coast hours. At least the traffic is easy, and I get home early and do a lot of surfing and kayaking. The only drawback is that I get to bed really early."

"I don't mind going to bed early." Hannah giggled.

"Here we are. My housemates are out on the beach. It looks like they are trying to get a windsurfer going. Have you ever tried?"

"Nun-uh. It looks really difficult with the waves. That's a hard pass for me. Do you have any snorkeling gear? I might do better with that."

Ronin's house was a three-bedroom beach bungalow rental that he shared with two other guys; one was a stock trader like Ronin. The beach house was seated on tall stilts so the tides and waves could wash under it without doing damage to the *hale* (house).

"Let me check the boat room for snorkeling gear. The tide's out, so it's actually a good time to get to the reef and see some yellow tang fish and maybe a *honu* (turtle) swimming around."

On the same day that Hannah left for the other side of the island, Tim rang the girls.

"Hey Jenae, it's Tim. I was wondering if you and Hannah needed me to drive you to the grocery store or anywhere since you don't have a car. I'm heading out to run some errands soon and thought you may need to pick up some things."

"That'd be perfect for me, but Hannah is on the North Shore with a guy she met on the plane. I'm not sure when she'll get back."

"That girl is such a tart. I reckon she's always been that way. Well, let's go out to dinner after shopping. How about you and I go on a proper date? Do you want to grab a bite to eat at the Hard Rock Café?"

"Sure, as long as we don't end up at a strip club again."

"We can save that for our third date." Tim felt excited as he put on extra deodorant after his shower and even gargled with mouthwash.

After sundry shopping, Tim and Jenae parked his truck in the garage at the Kaipuna condominium building where he lived. It was about a mile walk to the Hard Rock over the Ala Wai Canal Bridge and under the stars of a moonlit, balmy evening. They talked about their interests, and Tim mentioned that he and some Marine buddies had signed up to do the triathlon sponsored by their base in six weeks.

"I do like triathlons. I did one in college. As a kid, all of the neighborhood kids rode bikes twice a day to a local city park for morning and noon swim practices. I have two out of three sports burned into me from an early age," Jenae said.

"It sounds like you'd be perfect for it."

"My running kind of sucks, though, especially after a swim and bike ride beforehand. I run for fitness, but I'm still really slow, so basically, I jog."

The triathlon that she had done in college was a sprint. It was the shortest distance for a triathlon competition and consisted of a .5-mile swim, 12.5-mile bike, and 3.1-mile run.

"You should do it with us. You still have enough time to train, and you can help me become a better swimmer - that's my weakness."

"OK, but only if you take me bike shopping tomorrow for a road bike. I can ride it to work instead of taking a stinky bus."

"It's a deal. I'll take you where I got mine."

"Awesome, thanks. By the way, what are the distances of this triathlon?"

"It's Olympic length, which is a 1-mile open water swim in Kaneohe Bay, a 25-mile bike ride down toward Diamondhead and back, and a 6-mile run around the base."

What the hell? It's double my last race, but I like this guy, so why not? Jenae thought.

"I couldn't do it on my own, but training with someone will probably make it more doable. OK, I'm in."

Tim and Jenae walked back to Tim's place, and he invited her in to have a look around. The Kaipuna was a 34-floor iconic condominium built with an S wave, which gave every unit an ocean view. The patios were even curved, mimicking clamshells. Before reaching the entrance, Tim walked Jenae along the garden path and stopped at a decorative pond.

"Do you like it here in Hawaii so far?" He brushed her pinky finger with his hand. "Well, of course! What's not to like?" Jenae readjusted her front bangs behind her ear.

"Thanks for picking us up from the airport and taking me shopping and on a date tonight. It's been really fun."

"Can I kiss you, Jenae?"

Jenae stepped back and tilted her head with a smile. She was excited but reluctant to move so quickly with Tim. Their conversations came with ease, like they had known each other forever.

"OK, just give me a peck on the cheek." Tim tapped the side of his face.

As Jenae tittered, she stood on her tippy toes with her hands braced on Tim's shoulders. She could feel Tim's warm breath on her neck and the strength of his arms and back; she gave him a peck on the cheek. Tim turned his face to hers, and desire quickly took over for both of them and turned into a flurry of passionate French kissing like waves crashing on the beach. The craving retreated until the next ocean surge. They both laughed, a bit embarrassed, as their make-out session came to a temporary pause.

"Let me show you around," Tim said as he guided Jenae through the glass front door with his hand on the base of her lower back.

"What floor do you live on? I think this is one of the tallest building I've ever been in."

"My place is on the 12th floor, and it has a pretty good view. Celebrities live here, too; sometimes, you see them in the elevator. I think Higgins from Magnum P.I. lives in one of the penthouses."

Tim was tall with a strong chest and arms, and his legs were thin and tan. Jenae had taken note of his physique because he was always wearing shorts and a sleeveless singlet. Curly brown hair on top of his crown sharply contrasted the sides of his head, which were buzzed into a faded cut. He fit the stereotypical jarhead marine depiction; he even had a thick neck. His voice was unusually high pitched, not like a testosterone bass or even baritone, but possibly an alto. His teeth were straight and white, and he often licked his lips when he talked to Jenae.

Once inside Tim's one-bedroom apartment, he offered Jenae a beer in a longneck bottle. They sat out on the patio in metal chairs, toasting the beer bottles as lust bubbled up in both of them that couldn't be contained. Tim put his hands around Jenae's waist as they kissed, and in one swift motion, Tim lifted Jenae up onto the patio table. Jenae wrapped her legs around his waist without any hesitation. She didn't mind showing affection out in the open, even if they were in full view of Tim's skyscraper neighbors. *Nobody knows me, and I don't care if anyone sees us,* Jenae surrendered to ephemeral ecstasy.

Chapter 4

Waikiki

The first weekend in Hawaii exceeded Hannah's expectations. Friday afternoon turned into Saturday night, then Sunday morning. Hannah returned to the concrete hotel on cloud nine, in lust with a successful, good-looking man. Ronin was born and bred in the San Francisco Bay Area, which gave him an air of big-city sophistication to complement his tanned abs of an island god. When Hannah returned to the hotel on Sunday afternoon, Jenae was reading through travel activity books and had a big map of Honolulu spread out on top of her bed.

"Long time no see, roomie."

"I know; sorry about that, but I think I'm in love! Ronin is so cute and so nice. I really like his roommates, too. You should come with me next weekend, Jenae."

"Wow, it must have gone really well if you have plans to go back already."

"What did you do while I was away?"

"Ah, well, Tim drove me around to run some errands, and he took me to the bike shop so I could buy a road bike. He talked me into doing a triathlon with him and his buddies in six weeks, and I figured I could get some of my bike training in by riding to and from work."

"Where's the bike?""

"Tim let me store it at his apartment for now until you and I get situated permanently."

"That sounds exciting and exhausting. I'd never attempt a triathlon. But I know you're the jock in the group, so I'm behind you a hundred percent. By the way, while I was up at Ronin's place, I called the travel agency about what condo they would be putting us up in, and they said at a two-bedroom condo in the Kaipuna condos here in Waikiki. Isn't that where Tim lives, too?" Jenae's face turned red, and her heart leapt a little bit.

"Yes! Oh my goodness, this will be perfect. Tim can drive us to places that are out of walking and biking distance. Hannah, I do want to ask you, though, is anything going on between you and Tim? Do you like him? Did you date? I know you grew up with him."

"Oh shoot, no, we never *really* dated, and besides, I've fallen for Ronin. If you like Tim, go for it! He's a great guy, and he has a good heart."

———◆———

32

Jenae never revealed her tryst with Tim to Hannah, but Hannah began to have her suspicions. Jenae appeared too comfortable around him. They were always out training on bike rides or running to swim at the beach park. Hannah didn't know about their playful halfway make-out sessions during their evening swim either.

"So, how do you like work, Jenae? We've been at it for a week already. What do you think of your unit?" Jenae and Hannah relaxed on the balcony on the 16th floor of their new abode at the Kaipuna.

"For starters, the commute is a bit better than on the first day of riding my bike to the hospital. I feel like the bus driver who tried to run me over is starting to warm up to me and figured out that I'm not going away anytime soon. He gave me a wide berth and even waved at me today. I kind of feel accepted, but Queen's is different from Dallas because it's a smaller hospital. It has more of a community vibe. I'm used to the big medical centers like the one you work at now. The gals that I work with seem really nice, but I get the feeling that they don't want to invest time into getting to know me because I'll be leaving in a few months. It's understandable. My nurse manager gives me the death stare several times a day, but a girl on the unit invited me to her family picnic at Ala Moana Park on Sunday."

"Oh yeah? That sounds like a good chance to experience some Hawaiian culture."

"I don't know about learning about the culture, but the food should be good. Rhonda is a white girl and super nice.

She was raised on the west side of the island near a base; her dad is in the military or something. She has blond hair and blue eyes and the thickest Hawaiian accent of anyone there. She doesn't look like a Rhonda either," Jenae responded.

"And how's the NICU at Children's Hospital? It seems like you're gone more because you're doing five eight-hour shifts versus my four ten-hour shifts."

"I don't mind the five eights because we change it up between days and nights. That leaves my evenings free to go out, and I get weekends off too."

"I can't wait until Pami gets here. You're lucky you get to work with her. What's her hold up?"

"She said she is delayed because she needed to work a few extra weeks in San Antonio until the hospital could get coverage. She's planning on returning to that unit when our Hawaii adventure ends, so she doesn't want to burn any bridges." Hannah said.

"I'm jealous. I wish I had some friends from home at my hospital with me."

"I feel like we never see each other, Jenae. Do you want to come with me to the North Shore on Saturday to meet Ronin and his roommates?"

"Sure, that should work as long as I can be back on Sunday for the picnic with Rhonda.

"I heard Tim's Uncle Dingle is coming to visit him for a couple of weeks. I've met him a few times in Galveston, and he is a blast."

"Is that his real name? Dingle? It sounds like a derivative of dingleberry."

"I actually think it's a derogatory nickname given to him as a kid, and he embraced it. Oddly enough, it fits his personality. Dingle is a constant country comedy show. He has a million jokes and keeps everyone in stitches. He's kind of like an older brother to Tim because they are closer in age than Dingle was with Tim's dad. You know Tim's dad died at a really young age, like at forty years old."

"Oh my goodness, was he in a car accident?"

"No, he died of a heart attack because he had familial hyperlipidemia. His cholesterol was in the five hundreds on a consistent basis for his whole life; it's a genetic thing for sure."

"For real? God, I hope Tim is OK."

"I'm sure he keeps an eye on it, being in the military. Not to change the subject abruptly, but some of the travel nurses that I work with in the NICU are meeting up at Moose's for a late, happy hour. Should we go meet them? They've been here a few months already, and can give us ideas of where to go and what to see on the island."

After a quick shower and a change into peachy, flirty linen shorts and razorback crop top ensemble, Jenae slipped into her leather tie-up sandals and poured a light beer into a solo cup for the walk to the bar. Hannah wore stonewashed high-waisted jeans, with a white-T-shirt tied at the smallest part of her midsection. Her blonde hair was tied up in her signature side ponytail, and her eyes were painted with sparkly eye shadow to make her peepers pop. Jenae barely wore any make up except for face lotion, mascara, and lip-gloss because the sun had already given her a nice glow.

Hannah pointed to the beach just beyond Fort DeRussy Base on Waikiki Beach.

"I heard the girls talking at work that there'd be a beach volleyball tournament going on just over there this weekend. We should try to go before heading up to the North Shore tomorrow."

"OK, sure. I can't believe we've only been here a week. It feels like it's been a month already. Can it be possible to have too much fun?"

"Howdy, ladies!" Hannah announced their arrival to her co-workers sitting on stools at a high-top table. She was a little bit winded from walking up the stairs to the loft bar.

"This is my friend from Texas and roomie, Jenae. She is working at Queen's this summer."

"Hi Jenae! Welcome to our hangout. Moose's has the best happy hour and cover band – and the air conditioner is always extra cold." The waitress placed a plate of loaded potato skins with bacon bits and sour cream smack dab in the middle of the table. Jenae thought: *I'm starving; I could eat a whole plate of those.*

"Can I get a Long Island Ice Tea please?" Jenae asked the waitress. "It's two for one happy hour right now, so I'll bring you two," the waitress responded. "Bring me two also, please, and another order of potato skins," Hannah said.

The ladies traded nursing war stories and locations where they had traveled.

"I really loved Alaska last summer. There were so many great hikes, and the blooming wildflowers were an unexpected surprise. And I got a big incentive bonus for going there. I have no regrets whatsoever."

"My recruiter told me about Alaska too. It seemed very appealing, but my main goal for traveling is to spend time with my friends," Jenae said.

"Aw, that's sweet of you to say, Jenae."

"You know it's true, Hannah. I wouldn't be here if it weren't for you and Pami arranging the whole thing."

"Well, yeah, that's true."

"But now, it seems like everyone I know is planning a vacation to Hawaii and staying with me while I'm here. My brother, my mom, my dad, and a few different friends are all coming at different times."

"Oh yeah, get used to it. I have visitors every other week, too," said the workmate.

"I also foolishly signed up for a triathlon in July, which I need to train for. I honestly don't know if I have time to work." Jenae took a deep breath in and sighed. "Maybe I should've picked Alaska instead."

Just as the second tall, chilled alcoholic beverage hit Hannah's brain, the band started their first song, and Hannah sang along to Never Gonna Give You Up. I love this video. We could be Rick Astley's backup dancers. Come on, let's all get on the dance floor!" Hannah shouted with an extra twangy accent.

The evening stretched into last call, and the ladies parted their separate ways.

"Good night! We'll meet you at the beach volleyball tourney tomorrow at noon." Hannah and Jenae made it back to their condo slightly more sober than they started after the mile-long walk back from Moose's. Jenae retired to her big bedroom with an ocean view and a private bathroom. She scored the bigger bedroom because Hannah worked nights and needed the quieter room to sleep during daytime hours. Hannah retired to her back bedroom with barely a window. She had to pass through the galley kitchen and laundry closet to get there.

After her first good night's sleep in over a week, Jenae groaned as she rolled out of bed and into the shower. Hannah was in the kitchen preparing a toasted English muffin. She smothered it with butter and jam and poured a cup of coffee. Jenae could hear the scraping of the crust of the bread with a knife, and the aroma from the nutty cup of Joe made her mouth water.

"Hey, do you want some coffee, Jenae? We don't have much to eat in the fridge."

"No thanks, I'll just have a Diet Coke and some chewable Vitamin C. I picked some bottles up at the GNC last weekend with Tim. I should've asked him to take me to the grocery store."

She'd started her athletic diet plan that would help her shed some pounds before the triathlon. Jenae looked forward to her daily Chicken Fajita Pita with salsa from the Jack in the Box just around the corner from the condo. It was only 320 calories, which was a real splurge for a girl who had sworn off eating for the summer.

The beach in front of Fort De Russy was set up for the volleyball tournament, and the girls eyed a poster that advertised that a top-level men's team from California was expected in the final match. Sinjin Smith and Randy Stoklos were the favorite, but Karch Kiraly was in the mix, too. Hannah became a volleyball expert and fanatic in preparation for the event. She had a penchant for any kind of men's sporting events, especially ones with glistening muscles on display. Vendors were out promoting their wares before many spectators arrived. Jenae was first in line to get a semi-permanent stick-on turtle tattoo just above her hipbone. It matched her pink and black high hip-cut one-piece swimsuit. She made sure she was always wearing an athletic swimsuit under her clothes when she was out and about.

"Hey Hannah, I'm going to take a swim along the beach line until the volleyball game starts." Hannah had already settled into her low beach chair covered in Hawaiian Tropic tanning oil wearing a teeny flowered bikini and reflective sunglasses, with her face pointed to the sun.

"OK, I'll save your spot and wait for the other gals. I hope I don't fall asleep."

Jenae made a workout plan for the triathlon with Tim that required two disciplines a day, with a progression of distance each week. Swimming presented many easy opportunities as she carried her goggles in the fanny pack with her sunscreen. The hardest parts of ocean swimming were the gagging taste of salt water and not having big black lines on the bottom of the ocean to follow. Jenae had to learn to lift her head every dozen strokes to gauge her distance from the shoreline so that she didn't drift off course. Running was more challenging in Waikiki because there weren't any long stretches of pathways without having to stop at road intersections. Plus, it was just plain hot and sweaty. Biking to work was a nominal workout, just three miles each way. *I'll need a miracle to be able to finish this triathlon,* Jenae thought.

As she sauntered out of the ocean after her swim, Jenae struggled with sinking sand beneath her feet and waves hitting her from behind. She navigated the broken seashells on the sand and looked up to see a very tall, bronzed, blonde – haired man with a beard in a loincloth standing in front of her. His appearance and proximity startled her. His presence was halting and confusing. He smiled at Jenae and slowly walked away down the beach with his hair blowing in the wind.

"Hi, ladies!" Jenae greeted the nurses from the night before who were sitting in the sand with Hannah.

"I just saw the strangest guy on the beach over there. There he is." Jenae pointed toward him before he fell out of sight.

"Him? He's always around, and he usually has a few little guys walking with him. We call him Sand Jesus because he always looks like that with the tan loincloth and tie-up sandals, and he glows from the sun reflecting off of his oiled-up skin. He looks like he was formed out of the sand."

"Yeah, nobody that I know has ever talked to him, although we've tried. He's a man of few words, I guess." Sand Jesus was the closest Jenae and Hannah got to holiness the entire summer, although Jenae called out to God many times.

Chapter 5

North Shore

"I told Ronin and the guys that we'd drive up to their place at about five o'clock. I hope that's OK with you. Thanks for going with me this weekend. I'm going to rent a Jeep from the rental place around the corner; it's pretty cheap for the day." Hannah said enthusiastically.

"Ok, sure, that should work. I can pitch in for the Jeep rental. But, I might leave the volleyball tournament a bit earlier to take a quick roundabout run back to the condo before I hop into the shower. I'll plan to be ready by four-thirty at the latest." Jenae was obsessive about getting her workouts in and followed a strict schedule so she could survive on triathlon day.

A run down the Ala Wai Canal was the closest thing to a natural setting in Waikiki. The sidewalk alongside the shallow, thin waterway allowed non-stop jogging past an outdoor recreational area, where middle-aged men played baseball on a well-maintained diamond. The Iolani School was empty further down the strand, and weekend warriors played golf on a well-manicured course beyond that. Jenae turned around at the zoo at the entrance of Kapiolani Park and stopped to stretch at a traffic light. When the light turned green, she headed back up to the top of Waikiki in order to get back to the condo in time for their evening plans.

———◦———

The North Shore had a very different vibe from big, hot, Waikiki. A cool breeze after sundown chilled Jenae's exposed sunburned arms and legs. She grabbed a towel, wrapped it around her shoulders, and stayed close to a fire pit in the middle of the beach that the guys built just before their arrival. Jenae was a good conversationalist for the most part. She often bragged that she could talk to a brick wall on blind dates, which made her boring date feel like he was the king of the world, but not tonight. The guys Hannah had left her with on the beach while she was inside with Ronin were not Jenae's type. She had exhausted herself in just one week by working at the hospital, exercising, and attending social events, all while drinking booze with very little nourishment. There was no food at the supposed BBQ, only cheap beer, boxed wine, and a bag of greasy chips that Jenae couldn't stomach. All she could think about was a bed with a soft pillow under her head.

"Hey, sorry that I am so tired, guys. I had two workouts earlier today and a mentally taxing week at work. I think I overdid it."

"No worries." The roommates wandered off and pounded down a few Pabst Blue Ribbons. They couldn't care less about this chick that tagged along with Hannah. And they certainly didn't want to have to entertain her while Hannah and Ronin were catching up in the house.

Jenae tucked her legs underneath the towel wrapped around her in the Adirondack chair. She placed her forehead on her arms that rested on her knees and closed her eyes. Her rumbling innards didn't allow her to catch a catnap, but she still pretended to be asleep with her face buried in the towel to avoid small talk.

After the sun had been set for a few hours, Hannah reappeared on the beach with a big smile on her face, pep in her step, and her shirt on backward.

"Are you feeling OK, Jenae?"

"I'm just exhausted from all the excitement. Are you ready to head back to our condo soon?"

"OK, I guess so. I was hopeful we would stay a while longer."

"I really appreciate it. I hate to be a dud, but I think I'm still catching up on jet lag and all. I'm really struggling." Jenae slowly gathered her things with half-opened eyes and waved goodbye to the guys.

Sunday was a new day after eating a bowl of fruit, a cup of yogurt, and getting a full night's sleep. Hannah drove back up to the North Shore to be with Ronin, and Jenae wandered over to Ala Moana Park to join her new friend Rhonda for a traditional Hawaiian picnic.

"Aloha Jenae!" Rhonda said with a big wave and an authentic Hawaiian accent. Her thin, delicate build and blonde hair still threw Jenae off, but Rhonda was a true blue Hawaiian. Jenae felt honored to be invited to the family's weekly dinner on the beach. Rhonda's extended family picked a different beach each weekend to hold an after-church luncheon, and lucky for Jenae, this one was just down the road from her condo. A lot of island dishes – some repeated two or three times – filled the fold-out table covered by a red and white, checkered tablecloth. They had grilled chicken with Teriyaki sauce, grilled chicken with sweet sauce, grilled chicken with no sauce, traditional roasted pork, macaroni salads, potato salads, steamed rice, poi casseroles, rolls, POG drinks, and special papaya and pineapple rum cakes.

Jenae's mouth watered, and her tummy rumbled, but as she made her way down the line, all she could put on her plate were the three kinds of chicken wings and a dab of potato salad. The strict eating plan was retraining her brain to almost be afraid of carbohydrates.

Children played on the outdoor equipment and in the calm waters, where she and Tim had their swim workouts/make-out sessions twice that week. Conversations with Rhonda's mom, dad, aunts, and uncles easily helped Jenae understand how Rhonda developed her kind nature and relaxed vibe. It was foreign to Jenae, but she loved it and filed the experience in her brain for later, when she could create her own family traditions.

Chapter 6

Island Date

Tim rang Jenae on Monday evening to invite her out to dinner at the Marine Base the next day.

"They have Mongolian BBQ on Tuesday nights, all you can eat. It's really cool because you get to pick out exactly what you want, and the chef cooks it on the grill in front of you. Plus, it's really healthy with lean proteins and lots of vegetables. I want you to see the base, too.

"Sure, that sounds like fun. Can we drive the running route for the triathlon and have a look at the bay where we'll be swimming?"

"You read my mind," Tim said.

"I'll be off work at 5:30, so come to my apartment at about 6:15 to pick me up. I should be out of my scrubs by then." Jenae hadn't talked to Tim all weekend, so she was pleasantly surprised when he called her to go out. *I'm not sure if this is a real date or a triathlon buddy thing.*

Indeed, it was an actual date. Tim opened the door of his high-profile truck and held her hand as he helped her step up into the bench seat. Before he started the red truck, he shuffled through a bunch of CDs and asked Jenae what kind of music she liked. He opened the case and showed her his collection. "Here, look." Tim leaned in closer to Jenae.

"Why don't you slide down closer to me so that we can look together? Do you like Sting, Phil Collins, John Mellencamp, or Guns N' Roses?"

"I'm not into Guns N' Roses, but anything will do."

"That's too bad. Slash is my hero." They pulled out of the garage of the condominium with the windows down, the air conditioner blasting, and Jenae singing to "Cherry Bomb" by John Mellencamp. *Say yeah, yeah, yeah.* Tim bumped Jenae with his arm and gave her a smile with each flirty comment. Jenae loved the attention and couldn't believe she was one of those couples sitting close to each other in the cab of a truck. *Were they going to make out at the red lights, too?* Jenae was just a little bit embarrassed. As they escaped the concrete overpasses and exhaust fumes of the city, Tim pointed out the beauty of the Pali Pass. The mountain was nuzzled in a light rain cloud, and the electric green terrain radiated through the fog.

"There's a trail over that ridge. It can be slippery and dangerous, but a couple of my friends hiked it last week. I think there have been a few fatal falls from there recently."

"I'll skip that adventure, then. I'm not a mountain hiking girl." Jenae replied.

"You have to climb Diamond Head while you're here — everyone does it. The view is spectacular. It's more of an uphill walk, anyway. Hey, I wanted to take you out tonight because my Uncle Dingle is coming to visit for a few weeks, and he arrives tomorrow night. He may take up a lot of my free time while he's here. But if you want to get some girls together on the weekend, I was planning on doing an island circle tour with Dingle."

"Pami is coming in this week, too, so I don't know."

"Bring her and Hannah along; we'll have a blast. Hannah knows Uncle Dingle — she has met him a few times. We can start early and climb Diamond Head, and we'll end up at the pineapple fields. We can hit the best beaches in between."

Tim's cohorts smiled a little too eagerly as they greeted Jenae at the base restaurant. "It's nice to meet you too," Jenae repeated a few times. Tim was very attentive and helped Jenae navigate the food selection and grill and brought her a beer to drink with her meal after he settled the bill.

"I know we're on base, but the view of the lush tropical plants is amazing. I guess it's this way everywhere on the island."

"This side of the island has a more serene feel than Honolulu, but Waikiki has the nightlife and energy that I like. Most guys live in base housing here, but I moved out when I could, and I don't mind driving over for work."

A tour of the triathlon route included the calm waters of Kaneohe Bay and flat roads for the run through and around the base. Tim cleverly stopped at a scenic overlook of the bay and asked Jenae for another kiss on the cheek. She slid across the cab bench seat and gave him a tender kiss on the mouth. "I think we are past the cheek routine," she said. They snuggled, kissed, caressed, and laughed with passion. "Thanks for dinner. I'm having lots of fun."

Tim explained the bike route as they headed off base. "It takes us all the way back to Hawaii Kai, up over the cliffs past Hanauma Bay, and then back to the base. We can drive the route next weekend on the circle tour."

On the drive home, Jenae and Tim had more serious conversations, which included Tim's family.

"Hannah told me that you are close to Uncle Dingle and that your father died very young."

"Yeah, my dad had really high cholesterol and died of a massive heart attack when he was 40. It was a horrible time for my family. I was a freshman in high school at football practice when I got the news. The same thing happened to his dad.

"I'm so sorry that you lost him at such a young age. That must be so hard."

"My mom's been a huge strength for my younger brother and me, but I kind of carry the responsibility of being the oldest child. I check in on Walker, my brother, and send money to my mom every month."

"That's a tough burden. Do you know if you've inherited the gene?"

"I monitor my blood levels at the clinic, and it runs a little high, but not as bad as my dad's. I haven't determined if I have the exact gene, and don't know if I want to know right now.

That's one reason I signed up for this triathlon. I figure if I keep exercising, I may be able to cheat an early death. And it's easier to keep active when striving for a goal."

"We should have fun in the process, too. Which is also good for the heart."

"Thanks for training with me, Jenae. Life is short, and I'm going to make the most of it."

"Sure thing. My motto for my 20s is, 'I'll sleep when I'm dead.' Hopefully, this triathlon won't send me to my eternal nap before I'm thirty."

Chapter 7

Island Tour

Hannah visibly jumped up and down after she hung up the phone from talking to Pami.

"Pami's coming on Thursday. I'll borrow a car and pick her up from the airport."

"Perfect. I'll be at work all day, so hopefully, I can see her after I get home. Where's she going to live?" Jenae asked.

"That's the best part. Pami will be at the Kaipuna, too – just down the hall, on the 16th floor. The agency has her living with two other travelers. They'll be living in a three-bedroom condo."

"I wish the three of us could have gotten a condo together. Oh, well." Jenae walked to the balcony as she thought about Tim's touring plan for the weekend.

"I wonder if she will be up for the Circle Island tour with Tim and Uncle Dingle this weekend. Did you mention it to her on the phone?"

"Yeah, and she is excited to go."

"Awesome. Who gets to ride in the back of Tim's truck, since there'll be five of us?" Jenae asked.

"Oh, I can ride in the truck bed with Uncle Dingle. It'll be fun. You and Pami can ride up front with Tim. So, are you and Tim an item now? It seems like you're spending a lot of time together." Hannah said inquisitively.

"We're training for this triathlon together. The other night, he picked me up and took me to dinner. Afterward, he showed me around the base. I really enjoy being around him." Jenae didn't fully trust Hannah and was worried that she was possessive of Tim, even though she was head over heels for Ronin.

Pami came to the island full of energy and excitement, and an exploration excursion around the island was right up her alley. She got the best apartment, already had friends from home with lots of plans, and super new roommates.

The girls could hear Uncle Dingle's laugh from across the parking garage when the elevator door opened on the parking level.

"Are you ladies ready for an awesome day?" Tim asked.

"This is my Uncle Dingle. He arrived a few days ago from Galveston. And Dingle, this is the nurse squad, Jenae, Hannah (you know her from home), and I'm guessing this is Pami." The girls waved.

"Nice to meet everybody."

"How are your roommates, Pami? Too bad they didn't get a place for all three of you together," Tim said.

"I don't mind. The gals I'm sharing the condo with seem cool. Nurses are usually good roommates. I'm not much of a nature girl, but I'm ready to get this party started. I need to make up for lost time." Pami said.

"So, ladies, do y'all live here in the poontang building with Tim?" Dingle cracked himself up. "Well, isn't that what this place is? If I lived here, I would have *all* the good-looking girls visiting me."

Tim shook his head with a guilty smile. "You wish, Uncle Dingle."

"What does poontang mean?" Jenae asked.

"You don't want to know, Dingle has a dirty mind," Tim warned.

"Poontang–Kaipuna, it sounds the same to me!" Dingle laughed out loud.

They reached the starting trail of Diamond Head by 7:30 AM — on schedule for a cool climb to the top. The bowl of the ancient dormant volcano reached temperatures into the 100's for most of the day.

"When we reach the stairway, watch for climbers coming down because there's only enough leeway for a single-file line. There are 99 steps on this stretch," Tim instructed.

"How far is this hike up the volcano? It might be too much for this old fart!" Dingle shouted as he chased a gecko lizard across the barren basin.

"You'll be fine. It's only two miles at the most, and the breeze at the top will cool you down before the easy walk back down," Tim assured. The girls skipped to the top of the volcano and took pictures from the old turret structure, with Tahiti somewhere in the very far distance. The ombre turquoise colors started pale blue at the beach line below and deepened in color: Cyan, aqua, teal, cobalt, and admiral blue as far as the eye could see. Morning surfers carved their designs on white waves that moved them close to the beach before poetically duck-diving back into shallow waters and paddling out for the next swell.

"Look, we can see most of Waikiki from here. I'm going to learn to surf before I leave this island, just like the locals. It's beautiful!" Pami raised her stretched-out arms to give reverence to the Hawaiian Gods.

"Hanauma Bay and the Toilet Bowl are next after we stop for drinks and snacks at the convenience store. Grab a sandwich or something for lunch that will keep for a couple of hours. We'll stop at a beach and eat a little later," tour guide Tim announced. Visibility seemed forever in the clear blue water of Hanauma Bay as the clan snorkeled, looking at fishes and turtles weaving in and out of the coral reef and lava deposits. The coolness of the ocean was refreshing after the 4-mile hike on Diamond Head. Jenae and Tim stayed in the bay for a mini swim workout while the others headed to the Toilet Bowl.

With only goggles, the training pair swam freestyle stroke around the bay in a semi-snorkeling fashion.

"I had my land workout at the volcano, and I am counting this as my swim workout today!" Jenae shouted to Tim when she came up for air.

"I think that's fair. It's not bad taking in the island's beauty while we train. I think I saw at least a dozen different fish and two turtles," Tim replied. "I'm all for double duty."

Jenae splashed her heels up to solid land. Not many people knew about the blowhole, and the hike over the rough lava was a challenge for even the most agile. As they turned the corner on the jut out, they first saw Hannah in the middle of the large tide pool. She was flushing up and down as the waves rushed in and waned out. "Who's going to join me?" Shouted Hannah as she laughed and jostled in the waves hazardously close to the lava rock surrounding her. "Alright, let's all get in together," Dingle conceded. "It's nature's water park." The circle tour was already a success, and it wasn't even lunchtime.

"Where are we going next, Tim?" Hannah shouted over the blowing wind from the back of the open bed of the truck. Pami had joined Dingle and Hannah in the back so that she could get a jump start on her suntan.

"Down there is the From Here to Eternity Beach, but we're going to go down further because the surf is too big on this side of the island. I'll bring you back at sunset sometime to roll around on the beach in the waves." Tim winked at Jenae. "I see the red flags are out on the body surfer beach. It's really fun if you know what you are doing, but I don't want to kill Dingle on his big vacation!" Tim yelled out the back window jokingly.

In a private conversation in the truck's cab, Jenae queried Tim.

"I'm going to have to figure out where to take my brother, Niles, when he comes to visit in a couple of weeks."

"How long is he here for?"

"I'm pretty sure he plans on two weeks like Uncle Dingle. But I obviously have to work at the hospital because that is the reason I am here, right?"

"It seems like there isn't a lot of working between all of you nurses."

"Maybe not, but I have a feeling we put in more hours than desk jockey procurement officers," Jenae teased.

"Surely Niles can go to the beach and shopping on his own while I'm slaving away in paradise."

"After Dingle leaves, I have military exercises for a week with the Marines in California, so if you need to borrow my truck while I'm gone, you're welcome to it."

"Thanks, I appreciate it."

"I guess I'll be able to meet Niles at the tail end of his trip."

"Yeah, I can see you two getting along with your mischievous ways."

"What kind of name is Niles? British? Are you sure your family is from the Midwest? I know he isn't better looking than me, it's not possible."

"Ew, I never thought about my brother being good-looking until you made it awkward."

"I'll take you up on your offer to use your truck to pick him up at the airport. I have a feeling he'll want to head over to the other islands on my days off to look around. We should be around when you get back from California."

The big red truck stopped along the side of the road for the group to get a quick stretch break and walk over the rocky beach to take pictures of Manana Island. The huge rock in the ocean seemed close enough for a round-trip swim to Jenae. But before Jenae could suggest her bright idea, Tim encouraged a quick stop to avoid anyone getting into the dangerous waters. He knew about swimmers who got caught in the channel's choppy waters and strong current: never to return.

The CD player blasted a U2 favorite that seemed to match the beat of the wheels rolling down the two-lane highway. The rhythm flowed with the balmy air and waves of the Pacific. The moody music swelled Jenae's heart with feelings of love, or at least a moment of lust. Perhaps the title was more representative of their relationship; *I Still Haven't Found What I'm Looking For*.

"Gawd, it's such a busy summer. My younger brother, Walker, is coming back with me from California for the rest of the summer."

"Is he your only sibling?"

"Yep, Walker is a lot younger than me. It's like we were both only children in the same family. I had two parents raise me, but when my dad died, Walker was left with only a grieving single mom. He was so little when it happened."

"So, are you his father figure now?"

"I suppose I am on some level. But Dingle has stepped in as a dad for both of us."

"Walker just barely from graduated high school and has no clue what to do with his life."

"Does he want to go to college or a trade school?"

"He may want the college life, but his grades were so bad, and he's not cut out for it. My mom and I are just grateful that he graduated from high school; it was touch and go."

"Well, at least he graduated."

"For real. I don't think the military will take him with his dismal transcript, either. But he is a kind, sweet teddy bear with a big sense of humor, just like Dingle. My mom is hoping that I can give him some guidance while he's here."

"I'm sure you'll steer him in the right direction."

"OK, we're here! This is my favorite beach on the island. Welcome to Waimanalo Beach Park. I figured we could relax here for an hour or two. Watch your step around the monkey pods in the sand. It's like stepping on a pointy Lego if you get one caught in your sandal." Tim gestured at their feet.

"Hey Teeim, can you help me out of the back of the truck?" Hannah adjusted her bikini bottom before Tim picked her up and put her down on the sand by the wheel of the truck. "Isn't it nice having big, strong men around?" Hannah flirted. "Can somebody rub some sunscreen on my back? Not you, Dingle

— I know what you're thinking!" Hannah said jokingly as she shook the bottle in front of Tim.

Shade from the Ironwood trees blanketed the soft white sands for miles. As Tim and Dingle shoved the umbrellas deep into the sand close to the water, the gals shook their blankets and towels in the wind until they fell to the beach with a graceful landing; barely disrupting a few grains of sand onto their relaxation pads.

A gentle slope of the beach and low, slow waves made floating with toes poking out of the surface of the water feel like a spa treatment for Pami and Jenae as they caught up on life. They relaxed with their faces to the baby blue heavens, not rationalizing that their shoulders and noses would soon peel from sunburn.

"How is it working in Hawaii? Any major differences from Texas?" Pami asked Jenae.

"Nursing is nursing, but I've had some challenges fitting into the culture of my unit. I loved the women that I worked with in Dallas and San Antonio... obviously. Things are just different."

"How so?"

"It may be the actual physical environment of working in a smaller space. You know, everything is bigger in Texas. I have to fight for a place to chart, and moving beds around is more like bumper cars. Everything seems so cramped because it's an older hospital, and people are smaller, I guess. Not Amazonians like us!" Jenae laughed.

"I only get tiny patients in the PICU. And we confine them to a crib; it's easier to transport," Pami said.

"I'm just tired most of the time, and my patience wears thin with my nurse manager. She does NOT like me, or at least that's what it feels like."

"Focus on the fun. That's why we came!" Pami dove under the waves like a dolphin and popped up in a ridiculous pose.

They laughed hysterically, just like the old days, and stomped out of the ocean to have lunch with the others.

The final stop on the circle tour was the Dole Pineapple Plantation. The crew was tired, sunburned, and windblown, but they perked up when they saw a wooden sign at the entrance advertising Dole Whip. As they drove on the dirt road to the ice cream shop, a vast plot of land popped into view. It had rows and rows of pointy vegetation poking out close to the ground. "So, don't judge me, but I thought pineapples came off of trees. You know, like apples and pinecones do. I assume they don't. Now...I feel like an idiot," Pami reluctantly shared. "Nope, those are mature pineapple plants growing out there. Let's get our snack quickly because it gets boiling hot in these fields in the middle of the afternoon." Tim was tired and ready to clock out as tour guide.

As the red truck picked up speed on the highway back home to Waikiki, Hannah joked with Dingle about his dating life; Pami closed her eyes and visualized her first week in the PICU at her new hospital; Tim planned his shower and dinner of tuna and dill pickles; and Jenae worried about the calories in the Dole Whip soft-serve, dairy-free frozen dessert that she had just consumed.

Chapter 8

Oh Brother

Pami settled into her new routine and quickly thrived. The bus schedule was easy to navigate to the hospital, which was a straight shot down the road. One of her roommates was often found lying on the carpet of the apartment, crunching out her thousand sit-ups a day. The other roomie was at work or hanging out with her boyfriend or her brother; both were stationed at a military base nearby.

As Pami flipped a veggie omelet in a skillet on the stovetop, the smell of butter and slightly overcooked protein wafted from the kitchen. With a metal spatula in her hand, Pami looked like *Chef Boyardee* without the white hat.

"Do you want some, Jenae? I have more eggs that I can whip up for you."

"It smells delicious, but I'm allergic to eggs, remember? I'm going to head over to *Jack in the Box* and get my standard chicken fajita pita soon. It's the highlight meal of my weekend."

"Do you have any food in your apartment, or is it just chewable vitamin C wafers?"

"I would get more food from the store, but I can only put four plastic bags on the handles of my bike. And forget anything heavy like juice or milk. The last time I bought soda, it busted out of the bottom of the bag, and I had to leave a few cans that rolled down the crosswalk into traffic."

Pami lived a more normal life in Hawaii than Jenae. Pami was consistent with routines and she ascribed to three meals a day, work, very little physical activity, and partying on the weekends. She didn't need to do a rigorous sit-up routine because she had a tiny waist accentuated by her childbearing hips and stout legs. She walked like a proud Pomeranian with her chin up and a grin on her face.

"Where's Hannah been? I haven't seen her much at work. I guess we are on opposite shifts right now," Pami inquired.

"I hardly ever see her, even though we're roommates. She's been working nights and sleeps while I'm at work during the day. I'm always gone by the time she gets home. Plus, Ronin has that crazy schedule of trading on East Coast time, so I think it works out well for them to see each other."

"Hey, my brother Niles is coming to visit tomorrow for a couple of weeks. Tim let me borrow his truck while he's doing military maneuvers in the California desert. Do you want to come to the airport with me to pick him up?"

"Sure, I'll keep you company. Where's Niles going to sleep? At your place?"

"I don't know. I was thinking on the couch."

"Our third roommate has basically moved in with her boyfriend, so we have an extra bedroom that he can use here if he wants."

"That would be huge! Thanks for that. I think he wants to fly over to the other islands on my days off, so he shouldn't need it every night.

"You know us. We don't lock the door, so he can come and go as he pleases."

"Aloha, Niles!" Jenae smiled as she approached the baggage claim conveyor belt. She placed a puka shell necklace around his neck to welcome him.

"Hey! Thanks for picking me up and letting me stay with you." Niles gave Jenae a big brotherly bear hug. "Dang, it's HOT here. I can't wait to change into my swim trunks and hit the beach."

"The beach is always only a few miles away on this island. Meet my friend, Pami. Pami, this is my older brother, Niles."

"You're the first family member of Jenae's that I've met. I can see the resemblance," Pami replied.

"Well, we all look alike, so if you've seen one, you've seen them all," Niles chuckled.

"Pami has an extra bedroom in her condo right now, so you don't have to sleep on my couch after all. She's generously offered it to you while you are here."

"Awesome, I may need to extend my trip then. Thanks, Pami!"

As they loaded the luggage into the back of the big red truck, Niles patted his pants pockets front and back and then his upper shirt pocket.

"Shit, Jenae, before we leave, I need to find my wallet. Let me check my bags. I have my driver's license and my Discover credit card that I took out, but I can't find my actual wallet."

"I'm sure you'll find it tucked in a pocket somewhere," Jenae reassured him. The airport cop waved the big red truck out of the loading zone, and the three headed back to the Kaipuna.

Niles was a tall, handsome man who had all the girls in high school swooning over his long brown hair and flirty blue eyes. He was the rebellious second son, so everyone in the family was stunned when he married a girl from England on a ship docked in the Arabian Sea, but not as shocked as his fiancé in medical school waiting for him to return for their wedding. His deep-sea diving days ended soon after in a bends accident. He was underwater welding for oil rigs with one other guy for a record-breaking week, taking respites in a nautical bell. After the job was completed, they were brought up to the surface by the boat crew too quickly; the ascent time was miscalculated for the length of time they had been submerged at that deep level, and gas bubbles formed and got stuck in his brain. After years of recovery and becoming the father of two daughters, Niles came to Hawaii to look at the possibility of purchasing a dive boat. He wanted to set up a low-stress tourist business in order to get into a healthier place. He also wanted to break the cycle of frequent marital disagreements with his discontented wife living in the Midwest, far away from tea and biscuits.

"We can use this truck for a week while my friend Tim is away. I was thinking that you could show yourself around while I work the next couple of days," Jenae said.

"Sounds good. I want to see some sites around the island, like Pearl Harbor and some of the beaches. It's really nice of him to let us use it. Who is this guy? Are you dating him already?"

"I suppose so — we have a lot in common. Go easy on him."

"You know I can't do that, Jenae. What are big brothers for if not to scare off their sisters' boyfriends?"

"You've certainly perfected that."

Pami chimed in to change the subject: "Hey Niles, my friends from work are planning on going to a luau tomorrow night for kicks. Do you want to come with us?"

"Yes, you should go. Niles, I'll be working for the next few days, so this is perfect," Jenae said with relief.

"Ok, cool, do you think they take a Discover card? I need to find my wallet, dammit. Tomorrow, I'll call around and check into flights and scuba diving excursions for us next weekend if you're up for some island hopping," Niles said.

"Sure, that sounds fun. I'll get to finally use my PADI scuba certification in a decent spot. My open water dive was on a rainy weekend in Lake Texoma with an eight-inch visibility. I got well practiced with the compass." Jenae pulled into the Kaipuna parking garage. "This is it. Welcome to the legendary Kaipuna."

The next few days were productive and serene for Jenae. Pami entertained Niles for the most part; they went sightseeing, shopping, and snorkeling. It helped that he was staying at her condo, just down the hall. Jenae normally would have felt lonely with Hannah missing, Tim gone, and Niles playing long-lost brother to her best friend, but her introverted side was renewed with the peace of focusing on one thing at a time, with room to breathe.

Chapter 9

Ancient Voices of Lahaina

The airplane ride to Maui was a quick thirty-minute hop-over flight with beautiful views of the beach line and blue hues of the Pacific Ocean. Niles had booked an afternoon scuba dive with a boat out of the Lahaina harbor for that same day.

"We can fly and dive on the same day, just not dive and then fly on the same day. The pressures work against you." Jenae trusted Niles on anything related to scuba diving, especially after his accident. They drove their compact rental car past a field of sugar cane plants that were skewed toward the north by incoming trade winds. An antiquated, cream-colored tower in the middle of the field dispensed a wisp of smoke in the same direction. As they passed the neck of the island toward the head, Molokini and Molokai came into view at the top of a ridge.

"That must be the nature preserve that I booked to dive in today. Molokini is a volcanic crater barely above ocean level.

The aquatic life is supposed to be amazing." Niles pointed to the east.

"It looks really cool," Jenae said.

"Sorry I couldn't get you on the boat today. I weaseled my way on because I told the boat owner that I was looking to get into the business."

"No problem. I can check us into the hotel and get some lunch in town. I'll shop in Old Lahaina Town and hang around. I'll meet you at the marina when you get back."

"Thanks for understanding. I hope you're OK that I booked us for a boat and shore dive together the day after tomorrow."

"Sure. I'm looking forward to it. We can tour the island tomorrow, then."

The town of Lahaina maintained its charm and history of a whaling station. A museum at the harbor had large photographs of whalers proudly displaying the conquered humpback whales for their blubber next to wooden boats. Spears, nets, and grappling irons were attached to the walls of the original way station near the docks.

The ancient Banyan tree in the center of the square behind the museum was as majestic in the old-time pictures as in the current day, Jenae sat beneath it for a few moments of relaxation. As she lay on her beach towel and looked up through the branches of the primeval arbor, Jenae daydreamed about the Hawaiian rituals that unfolded in the coolness of the same darkened shade before colonists came. In her mind, music played on ukuleles, bold voices softly sang Hawaiian verses, hula dancers spun fire sticks leaving light echoes behind, and smoke arose from a roasted pig wrapped in banana leaves hidden underground in a pit oven filled with hot rocks. This was the peaceful paradise of Hawaii that she held in her heart.

"Hey there, sleepyhead." Niles looked down directly above Jenae's face.

"Oh, you startled me. I was just resting my eyes. How was Molokini? Are you ready to be a boat captain?"

"It was really cool. We dove into the crater and saw lots of fish in the sanctuary, but then went to the outer rim and saw a huge manta ray, bigger than my wingspan. Some turtles were hanging out there too. I'm wondering what the lifestyle is on an island this small?"

"It's a beautiful island, definitely a lot less hassle than you're used to."

"Yeah, I can feel the stress just melt off from my shoulders." Niles' eyes shined as he stared into the reflection of the lowered sun on the ocean.

"Do you want to grab some dinner? I hear music playing at *Fleetwood's* restaurant over there. Maybe Mick Fleetwood will be serving drinks behind the bar. I see your future, Niles... In fifteen years, you will be hanging out in Maui with the rich and famous." Jenae rubbed her temples in psychic mode.

"Maybe, but in the meantime, I need to figure out a new gig to put food on the table and make my wife happy. By the way, after calling home a million times, one of the kids found my wallet underneath the passenger car seat. I got my VISA credit card number so I can buy dinner."

"That is a big relief - at least one problem is solved! I'll pick up the check next time."

A guitarist accompanied a singer, tapping her leg and bobbing her head back and forth to the beat on the small stage at the restaurant. She started her set. *"This is for all of you dreamers out there."*

Niles was a generous soul, with or without riches. He showed external self-confidence, usually expressed through humor, but internally he held on to feelings of inadequacy. He often backed down to avoid confrontation with his wife, which was completely opposite from his rebellious childhood ways.

———◆———

Beep, beep, beep, beep... beep, beep, beep, beep. Jenae struggled out of bed to get to the toilet first and to brush her teeth and hair before Niles awoke. After she dressed, she pushed Niles' shoulder back and forth.

"Hey, wake up, Niles. It's your four AM wake-up call to drive to Haleakala Crater for sunrise. Remember? This was on the top of your must-do Maui list!" Jenae was dying inside as she rubbed her neck to calm down and wake up at the same time. "It's like being on the moon. Everybody says so."

Jenae rarely gave in to a change of plans once they were made, especially not for sleep.

"Ugh, I'm not going. I can't wake up," Niles said. "You go, take pictures." *Honk-shoo, honk-shoo.*

"I can't believe you! This was your idea." Jenae resigned herself to the fact that she was going to experience this glorious sunrise all by herself. She grabbed the comforter off of her bed, wrapped it around her shoulders, and rambled down the outside steps in complete darkness. "Unbelievable," she mumbled as she drove off into the pitch-black night.

Despite her insecurities in love, Jenae was an independent and self-confident twenty-six-year-old woman because of the way she was reared. Even though she grew up as a middle child in a large sibling group with two older brothers and one older sister, not to mention younger twin brothers, she always considered herself the smartest and most adaptable in the family. Her siblings wouldn't notice because she was invisible to them. She had to protect herself from aggressive situations from her siblings and from neighborhood friends. The rough-housing stopped when she turned twelve and grew taller, stronger, and became cleverer. Being in the middle of the pack meant never being old enough to go with the big kids, but old enough to do chores that the younger boys couldn't handle.

Eventually, Jenae found appreciation and attention from her large group of friends and their parents. Her independence arrived at age thirteen, along with her new light-blue ten-speed bicycle. As she drove toward the dormant volcano, her mind strayed to vivid memories of how she earned that bike... and her freedom.

She recalled how she and her sister earned the ten-speed bikes by spending one whole summer attempting to paint three outbuildings for their father. One garage housed the pool pump and equipment; one served as an abandoned wood shop, and another sheltered lawnmowers and rusty tools. As 100-degree temperature days piled up in August, Jenae and her sister spent more time messing around in the pool than wire brushing old paint off the siding.

"We're never going to get those bikes Dad promised for payment of painting this dang garage. I just can't do it anymore," Jenae complained.

"Dad's using us as slave labor. I think we've earned less than five cents an hour for this job so far. Let's confront him together and tell him that this paint job is as good as it's going to get." Her sister adjusted her paint-stained shorts.

"There's no way he is going to buy us those bikes; he's been bitching at us all summer to get this done. How're we supposed to do all this work? Scraping, sanding, caulking, and then putting two layers of paint on with worn-out brushes in the scorching sun. The paint dries on the brush before we can climb the ladder to put it on the wall." Jenae stomped off dejectedly.

The very next week, Jenae and her sister rolled their brand-new bikes off the back of the family's orange pickup truck. Even though the garage wasn't fully painted to their father's standards, he decided to reward their negotiating skills and relieve everyone's agony of attempting an impossible project. School was starting soon too, and they needed transportation that didn't rely on a parent driving them every morning.

"Girls, life's about pushing your boundaries and knowing what you can achieve. Find out not only what you're good at, but also what you enjoy. Part of this project was standing up for yourselves and negotiating for what's best for you. You showed perseverance, good job!"

Gawd, does everything have to be a lesson? Jenae lamented in her head about her psychiatrist father's words of wisdom. I bet he just made that last part up because he was tired of hearing us complain. This was the moment Jenae perfected her eye-roll. Bulge both eyeballs forward, look up to the right, then down to the left, then back up, and wait for the reaction. The eye roll was the closest thing to criticism she could do without saying a word. She used it a lot over her teenage years, especially with her father. He mostly laughed.

"Well, I learned that I'm not tradesman material. But I'm a pretty good negotiator. Maybe I'll be a lawyer," her sister bragged.

"I learned that I'll die if I don't go to college. I need an indoor job," Jenae said.

Daydreaming in the dark while she drove up the mountain alone was the only entertainment option for Jenae - not even the AM radio stations had started broadcasting at four in the morning. She stopped every half hour to check the map to make sure she hadn't made any wrong turns, which was almost impossible on an island with only two highways. She stopped at the only gas station along the way for a can of soda and a small bag of macadamia nuts; it was open early specifically for tourists ascending to the heavens of Haleakala. Halfway up the mountain, a light mist formed on the windshield of the car. *Oh, shoot, where is the lever for the windshield wipers? I can't see a thing through this thick fog.* With single-minded focus, Jenae clenched her jaw and slowly winded up the switchbacks, guided by the yellow lights on her rental car. She blinked her eyes a few times, attempting to get better acuity, but the blackness with ghostly white clouds swirling about the car refused to abate. *Is this hell or just purgatory before I reach the heavens?*

And just like God Himself snapped His Fingers, she popped out of the fog and into a clear black night with stars surrounding her. She could see reflections of other cars in the distance, but no people or lights. *Perhaps they're hiding in the warmth of their running cars and taking catnaps before sunrise.* The one-and-a-half-hour drive was just enough time to get situated before the grand event.

Jenae grabbed her camera, put a fresh roll of film in it, and chugged the rest of her morning soda. As she saw others emerge from their darkened cars with coats and blankets wrapped around their shoulders, Jenae braced herself and ducked out of the driver's seat with the hotel comforter covering her from head to toe with just her face peeping out. She followed the other gazers to the side of the abysmal crater facing east as a few sun rays appeared from below. A pointy lava boulder served as her pew for the awe-inspiring chromatic marvel.

"Ooh, ah," the scattered spectators gleefully whispered as the sun rose over the crater, creating a rapid change in the color scheme from brown to red to pink to orange and then to yellow. It happened so quickly that it could have been a scene opening for an epic 3D blockbuster. Jenae and her exposed cold toes in her sandals were thankful for the brevity of the event. She sprinted on the dusty rock roadway back to her car and cranked up the heat to thaw out from the 40-degree temperatures. *I hope the pictures turn out ok. The beauty of the colors against the crater will be hard to capture.*

The drive down the mountain was a direct contrast to the ascent. The bright sun allowed her to see the ocean all around, and the grasses alongside the two-lane road were green and lush as she navigated the turns with her foot tapping the brake to control the speed. *Oh shit!* Jenae unexpectedly slammed on her brakes as two colossal cows looking for breakfast trotted in front of her car and made her skid onto a thin dirt bank off the switchback. Her knees went weak, her legs shook, and her kidneys quivered as she gasped for what she thought would be her last breath. Half of her left rear tire caught air before she gained control again. In slow motion in her mind, Jenae pondered, *which would be the most painful death, blunt force trauma from hitting a cow or blunt force trauma from plunging down a 1000-foot drop?*

"Hey, how was the sunrise? Did you get pictures?" A very rested brother asked when Jenae returned to the room.

"You missed out alright. It was breathtaking in a lot of ways. I'll show you the pictures when I get them developed."

"While you were gone, I went out for a swim in the ocean. The surfers were out bright and early. Maybe I'll rent a board and give it a try later on. The waves look pretty tame off of this beach."

Jenae couldn't have cared less about Nile's morning swim. "I'm going to take a nap. Could you grab some pineapple and mango for me if you are going out? I saw a farmer's stand down the road."

"Nighty night. I'll come get you at noon if you aren't up by then."

"Good night. See you in a few." Jenae collapsed on her pillow.

Chapter 10

Maui Dives and Hula

The brother/sister pair drove around the north part of Maui in search of the perfect beach. Fleming Beach brought the biggest waves for body-surfing and had a reef further out with lots of board surfers. Honolua Bay was strictly for experts and dive boats.

"I heard a middle-aged local guy got gobbled up by a shark last week – right there at the mouth of that little stream." Jenae jolted Niles from studying a map.

"Bad luck. I suppose the shark was looking for food coming out of the stream," Niles contemplated.

"Dun, duh. Dun, duh. Dun, duh. You are gonna need a bigger boat." Jenae teased Niles about his tour boat business venture.

"I've encountered lots of sharks in my underwater welding jobs. You just have to worry when they start circling you for the third time. That's when you know you're toast," Niles said.

Napili Bay was their final stop, and they saved the best for last. A picture-perfect bay gave protection from huge waves, which allowed them to snorkel on the reefs. The soft sand entry was steep, created by sizeable tidal swings. A teenaged turtle stealthily surfed on the waves alongside young children sliding onto the shore. "Mom, Dad, watch me catch a wave!" shouted a thin, pale boy with a Canadian accent.

"Now, this is what I have always imagined Hawaii to look like." Jenae reached her arms straightforwardly and swept them open as if she were offering an embrace to the ocean.

"It's about time to head back to the hotel to get ready for our luau. I found some discounted tickets while you were sleeping this morning." Niles was pleased with his purchase because it made up for bugging out of the early morning sunrise expedition.

Lahaina Luau offered an amazing buffet of authentic Hawaiian dishes. Jenae decided that she should splurge for her first luau experience and try everything that was offered. No calorie counting on special occasions, especially with visiting family. The vibe was different, traveling with her brother. He had known Jenae all her life; he knew where she came from, and he always told her that she was the "lucky one" because she always won at card games. She wasn't going to be able to pull off the low-calorie diet bit with him, at least not on this excursion to Maui. The tropical cocktails with umbrellas and fruit condiments went down smoothly. They almost quenched Jenae's thirst like guzzling Gatorade on a hard bike ride, and they also gave her a warm buzz.

"I'm going to grab another drink. Do you want one, Niles?"

"Sure, I'm going to look around at the baskets and wood carvings. I need to get souvenirs for the family."

The drums beat, and dancers took the stage at sunset after the guests were seated with plates mounded with Huli Huli chicken, Kalua pig, taro root, green salad, Lomi Lomi salmon, Mac salad, Molokai sweet potatoes, Shoyu chicken, Poke, and sweet bread rolls. The feast was the centerpiece of the luau, and the removal of the pig from the underground sand oven by four strong young Hawaiian men signaled that it was time to eat.

Wahine (female) dancers in hula skirts with shell bras told whole stories with all-embracing body language. Their hips, legs, feet, arms, and hands gracefully swayed on stage – back and forth, back and forth. One story they told was about the journey on long, thin canoes across the ocean that carried islanders from different parts of the South Pacific to Hawaii to create a multifaceted culture. This luau was a celebration feast for the achievement of their ancestors for surviving the dangerous journey.

"Aren't you going to try the Poi? It is the famous dessert that Hawaiians love," Jenae asked Niles.

"I already did, and it's like tasteless liquid chalk to me. I'd rather have another fruity cocktail. I'll have to bring the family over to experience this if I don't decide to move here outright. The girls would love the dancers."

"Maybe I am wrong, but it seems like you're taking this time to reassess your marriage, too. Sorry if I am overstepping boundaries," Jenae said.

"It's a big topic, and you're right; marriage hasn't been smooth sailing for us. We probably fight because we aren't financially stable right now. I'm the breadwinner, and I haven't figured out my path forward yet."

"Besides being a boat captain, what else do you have your eye on?"

"I'm not sure what'll make my wife happy. Maybe if I go back to school and get my Ph.D., she'll respect me and love me more."

With a pained look on her face, Jenae placed her open palm on her chest.

"You know, Niles, you are good enough no matter what degree you have, how much money you make, or who says they're proud of you. You have to know that in your heart – unconditionally. You're good enough, and you do deserve love."

Niles nodded his head up and down, but he wasn't certain if Jenae was right or not.

"Look, here come the brave journeymen with big twirling torches." Niles pointed to the stage with water in his eyes. They watched in awe as the *Kane* (male) dancers illuminated the darkness with fire paintings.

"I want you to be really careful with who you have children with, sis. Don't be naïve like me. The responsibility is never-ending and limits your life. Don't get me wrong, children are the best thing ever, but know what you are getting into. Relationships, on the other hand, treat them like an employee – hire fast and fire fast. If it isn't good, don't delay, and move on so you can find someone worthy without wasting much time."

"But Niles, didn't you fire your fiancé at home too fast to impulsively marry someone else on a whim?"

"Good point. And that was a huge mistake to do it like that. I think about it a lot. I guess I was stressed-out at the time, and my emotions got the best of me."

"We're both suckers for an accent."

"Seriously though, I think it's a good thing that you are starting your MBA soon. You really need to find out who you are before partnering up with someone for life."

The evening ended in quiet contentment as they returned to their hotel room for a deep sleep before an early morning showtime for scuba diving the next day.

"Rise and shine!" Niles opened the heavy curtains on the salt-stained windows of the hotel room. "You get to go on your very first Hawaiian scuba dive, and I'll be your dive master. We're meeting at the Mala boat ramp just a bit north of here in a half hour, so let's get crackin'."

The shore dive off of Mala required putting fins, tanks, snorkel, and a mask on land as well as a walk backward into the gentle water lapping on the shore. As they entered the cool morning water with four other divers, Niles reminded Jenae not to touch any coral or plants.

"Fold your hands together at your waist like this." They slowly walked backward to a depth that would support their weight. The aqua adventurers sunk further under the surface, chin first and then mouth as they breathed through a regulator. After their masks were submerged, they swam toward the bottom of the sea in a prone, downward position, using only their legs assisted by big flippers attached to their feet. The motion was slow and deliberate, with their knees bending in an alternating rhythm.

Jenae surveyed the sandy bottom of the ocean bed while she swam closer to a shallow reef. Niles gave her an OK sign with his right hand, and she responded with an OK sign in return. He stretched out his hand and waved her in his direction. The sunrise above was creating beams through the waves to the white coral below. Colors changed from light blue to clear to yellow in big spheres at just twenty feet below the surface. She could hear only muffled sounds, but could see lots of bubbles rising from her breathing apparatus. She was immersed in a 360-degree dimension. Niles waved her toward his direction again and pointed to the coral below. Jenae couldn't see what he was motioning toward. Then he put his hand just outside a gap in the rocklike structure, and a creature jumped out and tried to grab his wriggling finger. The creature had a thin face with jagged teeth; the length of the body was unknown because most of it was inside the coral reef. Jenae startled backward and let out a muted squeal when a dark green spotted eel popped out.

As Jenae turned to swim back to shore with the group, she caught a glimpse of a baby turtle waving his front legs up and down and kicking his hind legs front and back in an attempt to catch up with its mama. Mama turtle looked back over her shell and floated until the baby honu reached her prehistoric-scaled tail.

"How did you like your first ocean dive?" Niles and Jenae walked up the rocky shoreline with tanks on their backs. Jenae flipped her pink and translucent fins back and forth, one in each hand.

"It was so much better than my open dive in Oklahoma. A whole new world was opened up to me. I felt like I could see forever under the ocean."

"Visibility is 100 feet right here, which is the highest rated, but I suppose it seems infinite after being in a muddy lake. Wait until the boat dive after this. Hopefully, we'll go to a bigger reef and see more underwater wildlife."

The small dive group piled into a rubber, steel-bottom Zodiac boat at the Mala Ramp, which was an obscure cement slope protected by a small levy. The boat was stocked with fresh oxygen tanks and a cooler full of sandwiches and canned drinks for lunch after the second dive.

The boat captain gave safety instructions on life jackets and signals while in the water.

Use the OK hand sign, which alternatively means flying asshole in Europe, to indicate everything is all right.

Use the wishy-washy hand sign for there is a problem and point to the problem.

The OK sign above the water is done with arms overhead formed in an O or with one arm up touching the top of the head.

Waving one hand in the air means there's a problem, so don't wave "Hi" to passing boats; maybe give the Chaka sign instead.

Thumbs up means go up to the surface - and return to the boat. Thumbs down means going down on the dive with your buddy.

"Everybody, go over the signs with your buddy so that you can communicate the entire dive. Don't let your buddy out of your sight and keep an eye on your dive watch for time. We'll be down for twenty minutes. When we give you the thumbs-up sign, it means go up now... it is not a suggestion. Your tanks are full, and we are diving 50 feet to the reef below, so be aware of currents. We'll be watching you. Safety first, but have fun," the captain commanded.

Niles demonstrated the proper way to fall backward off of the side of the boat, holding his mask as he rolled into the water, head and shoulders first. It reminded Nurse Jenae of the position most newborns are in on their entry into the world from the womb – albeit less squeeziness. She sat on the rubbery edge as she struggled to put her pink fins on over her diving booties. She pulled on her matching pink and white diving gloves and spit into her mask, rubbing it around to clear the fog on the glass.

"Are you ready to get in the water?" The boat captain asked.

"I think so. I've never entered the water this way. This is my first boat dive," Jenae replied.

"Here, let me give you one more spray to clear your mask before you go. Remember to breathe through your mouth."

"Ok, here goes nothing."

"Hang close to your buddy. We'll see you in twenty minutes!"

Splash! Jenae tumbled backward and found herself three feet under the surface before looking up and seeing Niles with a flying asshole sign. She righted herself, gave the OK sign back, and they descended to the reef below next to the underwater caves formed by lava tubes. Both Niles and Jenae moved their jaws around to pop the pressure that built up in her ears. *This is so exciting,* thought Jenae. *Oh, look at that school of pink fish with big eyes.* Jenae caught Niles' attention and motioned to look by pointing to both eyes and then in the direction of the cluster of fish sucking greens off of the rocks. In the next moment, yellow and black clown fish popped out from behind the cave, and a school of pale blue and yellow striped minnows scoured a reef colored with orange and red coral. Niles motioned her to swim closer, and he handed her a baby octopus whose head and body mostly fit in her pink and white-gloved hand. Jenae was careful not to squeeze it but to guide it while she observed its eight tentacles with small suction cups floating around her arm. Its brown and pink body didn't seem bothered by the attention.

Niles pointed to his watch and then to the cave. Jenae followed his rhythmic flutter kick as they turned the corner. Immediately she noticed a manta ray flying into the darker blue ocean by gracefully flapping its fins that looked like wings. A spiny string tail twice the length of its body floated in a perfectly straight line behind it.

As they entered the cave, Niles found another brown eel in an S-shaped curve coming out of the rocks, either recoiling in fear or ready to strike.

The tube was large enough for three people to swim shoulder-to-shoulder with tanks, but the current was swift and pushed the divers back and forth in the turbulence. They had to be careful not to bump up against the jagged rocks.

Once through the cave, orange sea urchins dotted the sandy bottom. Grains of white sand swept off of the ocean floor from the rapid, unremitting current. A full-grown turtle lounged in a large rocky part of the reef, which sufficiently camouflaged it from predators.

Jenae and Niles tapped their watches and gave the thumbs up to ascend to the surface. They swam slowly in a diagonal route toward the boat's diving buoy and flag. Jenae followed Niles' lead on the ascent. They paused for a minute halfway up to clear their ears and depressurize, just in case they exceeded the time limit. As they pierced the surface of the ocean, another diver shot up next to them in large bubbles as if a whale had exhaled underneath him. He ripped his mask off, spit out his regulator, waved his arms overhead, and shouted at the boat in a shrill voice.

"Help! Help! My girlfriend is caught in the cave." His breath was bursting in and out. "I couldn't get her tank loose from the rocks. She's stuck. Hurry!"

The boat captain quickly donned his jacket, tanks, and fins and pointed to Niles. "You come with us. How much air do you have?" "I should have enough; I'll swim on the surface to the cave and then dive from there." Niles' heartbeat raced as he sprinted to the proximity of the cave from above. The captain was already nearly to the cave with the boyfriend when Niles dove down to the trapped girl. She appeared oddly calm, but her eyes were wide, and her hands trembled when she pointed to where her tank was stuck in a crevasse.

The captain looked at her regulator pressure and quickly calculated that she had about fifteen minutes of oxygen left at that depth. He swam around her back and signaled Niles to help try to jimmy the tank from the rock formation. The captain gave a fist signal to stop and then gestured for the girlfriend to look at him. She had tears welling up in her eyes that made the captain's heart sink.

Niles signaled to start buddy breathing to the captain while he unhooked her vest and tanks. The captain took a deep breath from the regulator and handed it to the girlfriend. She took out her mouthpiece, put the mouthpiece from the captain in her mouth, and breathed in while he held his breath.

After three inhalations, she gave it back to him while she held her breath.

As Niles was able to release the girlfriend from her vest and tanks, the captain signaled to the girlfriend thumbs up and a buddy breathing gesture. She was released from her potentially watery grave. The captain and the girlfriend alternated breathing from the shared regulator, just as was practiced in her scuba class. They ascended to a decompression level for a few minutes while Niles followed in support. As they reached the surface, she gasped for air, and tears rolled down her face.

"You are fine. We've got you." Her boyfriend was crying just as hard as she was when he pushed a flotation device toward her. "Oh, Thank God!"

Chapter 11

Brother Walker

The events of the Maui visit gave Niles more to consider before investing in a tourist dive boat business. His experiences as a commercial diver presented many more dangerous predicaments than the girlfriend getting her tank stuck, but the seriousness of the situation did not escape his pro-con list. Jenae felt relief when she and Niles made it back to Honolulu in time for her scheduled shift. She found herself hustling back to the airport the next evening after work.

"I'm going to pick up Tim and his brother up from the airport," Jenae told Niles.

"What is his brother's name?"

"Walker, I think. He just graduated from high school and will be spending the summer with Tim while he figures out what to do next."

"I would ask you to navigate for me, but there's only room for three in the cab of his truck."

"No problem. I'll just hang out and make some phone calls."

Tim was happy to see Jenae at the airport after his weeklong training in California. He gave Jenae a big hug and introduced his brother.

"Walker, this is Jenae. She's the girl I told you about. We've been hanging out, and we're doing the triathlon together. She came out for traveling nursing with Hannah.

"Oh yeah, I know Hannah really well. We all grew up together," Walker said.

"Jenae, this is my little brother, Walker. Well, not so little in size, but my younger brother."

Walker's big, sunny personality matched his smile and stature. He had curly blonde hair and a baby face on a 6'4" frame.

"Nice to meet you, Walker. I love your curly blonde hair. Are you excited to spend the whole summer with Tim?"

"Heck ya. But mostly, I'm glad to be finished with school. I'm not looking forward to sleeping on Tim's couch, though; I guess beggars can't be choosers."

"It is a pullout couch, Walker. So, technically, it is a bed," Tim corrected. "Mom would have a hissy fit if I put you on a couch all summer."

"OK, do you have all of your bags loaded up? Tim, you can drive your big ole truck back home. It was really hard navigating the curbs. Good thing it has big tires," Jenae joked.

As they drove on H1 to Honolulu, Jim asked,

"So, did your brother make it for a visit this week?"

"He sure did. He's staying in Pami's condo on the other side of the building. One of Pami's roommates packed up everything and took off. So far, no other travelers have taken her place. So he's staying in the spare room over there."

"Lucky him," Walker muttered.

"Thanks for letting me use your truck this week."

"No problem. Thanks for picking us up. Were you off work today?"

"No, I had a short shift. We got back from a dive trip in Maui last night. It was very exciting. A girl on our dive boat got stuck in a lava tube, and Niles helped rescue her."

"Oh shit, that sounds scary."

"It was, but it turned out OK in the end."

"Well, that's good. Did you take any underwater pictures? You know they make the disposable cameras for that now," Tim asked.

"Sure did. But not of the stuck girl, silly!"

"I didn't mean that."

"I held a baby octopus. When I get the pictures back from the drugstore, I'll show you. Hopefully, some of them turned out."

Tim parked in his designated spot on the second level of the Kaipuna garage.

"This looks like a nice building, Tim. Uncle Dingle told me that it was close to everything in Waikiki. So, can I walk to the beach and shops from here?"

"Sure can, and it's a good thing because I have to work a regular tight schedule for the next few weeks. I won't have as much time to spend with you right off the bat, but it should loosen up after that. I hope you don't get bored."

"Walker can hang out with Niles and me when I'm off work," Jenae said.

"Yeah! That would probably be more fun anyway, Tim."

"Probably so. I can't wait to meet Niles. He sounds like a cool guy," Tim said.

"Me too," Walker chimed in.

After work, the gang of four, Jenae, Niles, Tim, and Walker, strolled to Ala Moana Park for a swim workout between the reef and the beach. The park wasn't crowded in the evening time and the water was calm. Further down the shoreline, a group of fit young twenty somethings were doing an aerobic routine with an instructor and a camera crew. The instructor was tall, dark, and fit. He shouted out commands to a recorded song as his troops stepped left, right, left, right for the warm-up and then down, up, down, up for burpees. The choreography was not the typical dance moves performed by middle-aged women at the YMCA.

"It looks like they are taping a show over there." Jenae pointed to the group.

"Yeah, that's Gad. He produces a workout series on TV based on his training in the Israeli Army. I'm pretty sure he was a commander," Tim said.

"Tim, weren't you on that show before?" Walker asked.

"My marine buddies were asked to do a class, and I got my fifteen minutes of fame, I suppose. He only asks super-fit people to do his workouts on camera. I've got it recorded on VHS if anybody wants to see how it's done." Tim flexed his muscles in different poses and laughed at himself.

"Absolutely," Jenae said,

"Can't wait... NOT," Niles laughed.

"Our episode was shot on the base, but he films from different locations around the island. They're out here on the point a lot. I think he lives in our building as well," Tim said.

The four entered the water, cleared their goggles, and started to swim freestyle in a group. Jenae and Tim practiced staying the same distance from the shoreline by lifting their heads out of the water every few strokes. Three-quarters into the planned workout, Jenae playfully grabbed Tim's ankle and pulled him back as she swam so that she could get to the lead position. Tim, in return, dove under her, grabbed her body to his, and rolled in the warm waters. They laughed as they surfaced, and Jenae dunked Tim's head underwater a few times until he got to a spot where he could stand on the bottom. She tried one more time by pressing down on his shoulders when she met the full resistance of Tim's strong body.

"If you can't dunk me, you are gonna have to kiss me," Tim teased Jenae.

"Nuh-uh, my brother is just ahead of us. And your brother, too," Jenae resisted.

"Come on, they can't see me taking off your swimsuit underwater, though."

Jenae pulled the string on Tim's waistline, undoing the knot in his swim shorts.

"I guess they can't see me taking off your trunks either."

"Jenae, don't do anything with those trunks, or your brother will know we are up to hanky-panky."

The outdoor beach shower allowed Jenae to straighten out her swimsuit. She and Tim ambled up to where Niles and Walker were sitting on a bench, drying their hair with beach towels.

"Hey, what happened to you two? We've been waiting here for a while," Niles asked.

"We were doing some extra drills to prepare us for the triathlon swim." Tim wiped his face, trying to get the grin off of it.

"Walker's been telling me about Texas and leaving his girlfriend behind. He's a good-looking young buck. He'll have lots of girlfriends in the future," Niles said.

Walker smiled and shook his head sheepishly. "Man, I hope so."

The inlet was a bit choppy, but Jenae had procured Kamaaina discount tickets for the four of them at a Jet Ski outfit in Hawaii Kai. It was a good break from work for Tim and Jenae and a fun activity for their visitors, Niles and Walker. Four jet skis were secured on a floating platform in the middle of the bay, and a young surfer dude named Kahi stood at attention and waved as the transfer boat arrived with its passengers. As Kahi took the hand of Jenae to help her on the platform, the men of the group scampered to the side of the boat one by one and jumped on the floating stage, causing a rocking motion.

"Easy guys! Am I the only one here who has never jet skied before?" Jenae asked.

"Yep...sure are... we go out in the Gulf of Mexico all the time," Walker said.

"I guess I'm going to need some extra instructions from Kahi then," Jenae said mischievously.

"OK, I'll meet you out there. Who wants to race me?" Niles asked.

"NO RACING! Stay on the figure eight and look out for boats and swimmers," Kahi warned.

The guys were off and running with rooster tails in their wake. Jenae took a few falls off the water motorcycle before she got her balance and the feel for turning without tipping over. *Forty-five minutes might be a little bit long for this activity,* Jenae thought. As she picked up moderate speed, Tim pulled up next to her and smiled. "Are you getting the hang of it?" Jenae smiled back as Niles and Walker flanked her on both sides at top speed, leaving her in choppy water. "I hate all of you!" Jenae screamed in the breeze as she wiped out in their wake.

The guys were standing on the platform, drying off as Jenae approached cautiously. She heard Niles say, "I need to change out of my swim trunks. My jock itch is going to get worse if I don't. Walker, hold this towel around my waist while I change." Walker held the towel at the small of his hip and looked away while Niles pulled down his swimsuit. As Niles stood up, the ocean breeze turned into a trade wind and lifted the towel above his head in a Marilyn Monroe moment. They struggled with the towel, trying to readjust it without success, while Jenae cried with laughter from the seat of her jet ski. Walker stepped away, held the palms of his hands over his eyes, and laughed, as Niles stood there naked while perched on his floating pedestal in the middle of the ocean. "That's called instant karma, brother," Jenae cheered gleefully.

Niles, Pami, and Jenae waited for Tim in Pami's condo, drinking a few beers and a bottle of wine as a pregame for a night out in Waikiki. Not that they needed a reason, but the party was to celebrate Niles last night in Honolulu, and the plan was to meet up with work friends at Moose's that evening.

"I'm going to miss this place, but I think if I moved here, it would kill me." Niles offered his glass for a toast.

"We do burn the candle at both ends, some more than others – Jenae," Pami said as she snacked on a Wheat Thin with a slice of cheese.

"This lifestyle is great for singles, but I can't see incorporating a family here with two young children. It's too far from family support," Niles realized.

"We're young and single and I live by the motto 'I'll sleep when I'm dead.' It's hard not to feel like sleep is a waste of time when the sun and waves are always out for the taking," Jenae replied.

"Not me. I am fine getting my eight hours of shut eye every night," Pami replied.

"You've always been the sensible one, Pami. Nothing ever flusters you," Jenae said.

"I can't work with a straight head without sleep and nourishment," Pami responded.

"So, what do you think about Tim and Walker?" Jenae asked Niles.

"I've had a lot of fun hanging out with both of them. Tim is nice, but Walker is way more entertaining. Walker and I spent more time together while you and Tim were working. He may not have a lot upstairs, but he's funny as shit and has a heart of gold." Niles chugged the rest of his beer.

Jenae was surprised that Niles didn't give more approval to Tim. Although her dating style was carefree, she still evaluated each of her relationships with marriage in the back of her mind. She wanted a crushing love but didn't think she would find it. Deep down she felt that she would have to settle and just take what she could get.

"Too bad Walker isn't old enough to come to the bar with us. Where's Tim, anyway?" Pami asked.

"I think he's on his way after he gets dinner with Walker. If you want to go now to meet the other gals there, I'll wait for Tim and we can catch up." Jenae picked up the phone to call his number.

"That sounds like a plan. Pami, you and I can catch a cab and we'll meet you there," Niles said.

"You're so lazy! It isn't even a mile walk," Jenae said.

"Your odometer is off Jenae. Everywhere we go, you say 'it's just down the street,' or 'it's just a mile walk.' What you really mean is that it's a fucking jog," Niles said jokingly.

"Alright, alright. Go get your cab and we'll meet you there. We'll probably beat you there walking because the traffic is so bad."

Moose's was hopping with a big crowd and the cover band playing current hits from the 80s. Tim and Jenae walked around the bar to look for Pami and Niles, but found it difficult to see anything through the dark smoky haze and the mass of humanity vertically squished together. The air conditioner wasn't keeping up with the large collection of 99-degree bodies amassed in one room. As they rounded the bar, Jenae felt a tap on her back and she turned around.

"Hey, what took you so long? I was kidding that Tim and I would beat you here," Jenae said.

"We had the taxi drop us off at another bar across the street and had a drink to give you guys some time to catch up to us." Niles felt someone bump him hard on his back.

"Damn! That girl just fell into me and spilled coffee all down my back!" Pami spun him around, had a closer look, and noticed wet yellow chunks at her feet.

"That wasn't coffee, Niles – somebody just vomited on you," Pami shouted over the crowd's blare. "Disgusting! Now what am I going to do? I doubt a cab driver would let me in his car smelling like puke." Niles walked away to gain his composure. Pami followed him down the steep stairs of the bar with her hand over her mouth, holding back her laughter. Within a few minutes they reemerged from the first floor with Niles sporting a Moose's t-shirt, compliments of the bar manager. Niles had donated his original tropical button down to the large trashcan inside the men's bathroom.

The going away party ended at 2 AM at an underground bar with a peep show enterprise next door. Jenae and Pami slipped into a video booth with short velvet curtains and plugged coins into a machine with a six-inch black-and-white screen. It reminded Pami of viewing microfiche documents in the public library. They giggled cheek-to-cheek to see the screen as fifteen-second clips of soft porn played with each dime inserted into the slot. The gals never got to watch actual porn acts because they only invested fifty cents before they got bored and returned to the bar next door with Niles and Tim. "Ah, what a disappointment," Pami said.

"I am not counting that as my first porn experience... I can see more on the beach or at the hospital than what we saw in those video clips."

Jenae would normally be embarrassed about goofing around trying to watch porn. But this night she felt carefree and irresponsible and that was OK with her. It gave her a broader perspective on what life was really about – being happy.

Chapter 12

Breakdown

Sirens from the fire alarm blared at 2:30 in the morning, which sent hundreds of residents of the Kaipuna on a downward trek in the stairwells to the parking garage below. The adrenaline rush this time was lessened, and the speed of her descent was slower, because this had been the third fire alarm in the middle of the night that week.

In a half-awakened stupor, Jenae thought, *At least I can count the stair climb back up to my bed as a mini workout and it won't hurt because I'm still asleep.*

Niles was back at home with his family on the mainland. Hannah and Pami presumably were working a night shift because Jenae didn't spot them in the garage. Tim and Walker most likely slept through the alarm or chose to ignore it. As soon as Jenae scampered down thirty flights of stairs in her pajamas all by herself, an all clear was given over an intercom to return to their apartments.

Between the prank fire alarms in the middle of the night and the construction of a hotel around the corner that started at

4 AM on weekdays, Jenae hadn't slept well in a few weeks. Drinking late at the bars didn't help her slumber, either. Many times she dizzily rode her bike to the hospital only to face the ten-hour shift in complete exhaustion. She also had a nasty yeast infection in her private parts that hurt her perineum every moment she rode on her twelve-speed bike. Nurse Rhonda gave Jenae a gynecologist recommendation who was willing to fit her into his busy schedule. She couldn't wait much longer to extinguish the fire that was burning in her bike shorts.

"So Jenae, why did you come to see me today?" The grey-haired gyno asked.

"A couple of reasons: First, I'd like to get a regular pap-smear, pelvic exam, and I need to renew my birth control prescription. Also, I think I have a yeast infection."

"I see. We can do all that and I may check for some other things too. Are you sexually active?"

"Yes, I'm seeing someone here."

"Do you use a condom in addition to birth control pills?"

"No, not usually."

"Ok, you're a nurse, so you know the risks of getting a sexually transmitted disease without using condoms?"

"Of course I do, but I'm pretty confident I'm the only one in my guy's life right now."

"My nurse will be in soon. Undress, put this gown on, and I'll be back to do your exam. You can put this sheet over your legs while you wait."

As the doctor warned her about the cold speculum, Jenae asked another question to distract her from the discomfort of the swabbing and the awkwardness of the exam.

"I'm having trouble sleeping at night because of noise from the construction outside. With the windows open all the time, I can't sleep through the jack-hammering that starts at 4 AM."

"Uh, huh. Where do you live?"

"In Waikiki. We've also been having fire alarms going off in the middle of the night for the past two weeks. I assume they're pranksters, but the management is adamant on the intercom to evacuate the building each time. After the adrenaline rush of running up and down stairs, I barely get back to sleep before the trucks start roaring again."

"That sounds frustrating."

"For sure, I'm stressed out that I can't sleep. And I'm exhausted at work."

"I can give you a sample prescription for a few sleeping pills to help you through the construction noise. You should be able to wake up if a real fire breaks out."

"Thanks, I'll give it a try. I don't like taking medication, but I'm pretty desperate at this point."

"OK, I have the specimen sample that I need. You do have some kind of infection going on down there. I'll look at it under my microscope really quickly and give you a result. You can get dressed and sit tight right where you are."

Wow, that's amazing that he can read his own slides and doesn't need to send them out to a lab. That's a first for me. Jenae wiped the KY Jelly from between her legs and threw the robe in the hamper next to the door. She was dressed and perched at the end of the armchair when the doctor reappeared with a concerned, if not disapproving, look on his face.

"I didn't see an overgrowth of yeast, but I did determine that you do have a chlamydia infection."

"What?" Jenae shook her head as her face flushed red.

"I've seen quite a lot of these infections this year. Hawaii is having an outbreak of STDs right now. Chlamydia is the most common culprit."

"I didn't see that coming." Jenae felt as if a rock had landed in her stomach.

"I'll give you a prescription for you and your partner and both of you should be fine. But no sexual relations until you've completed this course of antibiotics and you aren't having anymore symptoms like pain, redness or discharge."

"Of course, I'll take the entire prescription." Jenae sheepishly rubbed the back of her neck.

"Write your boyfriend's name down, and I'll give you medications from our clinic before you leave. Make sure he completes the antibiotics, too."

"Ok, will do." Jenae pulled her legs together with her chest caved and her spine bent forward as she wrote out Tim's full name.

"And, if you remember anyone else who you may have had sexual relations with, you'll need to contact him so that he can get tested and treated as soon as possible. Men don't notice the symptoms as much as women, which is why it's spread so easily."

<hr />

The bike ride from the doctor's office was contemplative and painful on her raw vagina. She stopped at the local grocery pharmacy to get her birth control pills and a topical ointment to ease the pain. *At least the doctor gave me the actual medication for the STD and some sleeping pills.* Jenae thought to herself. *I wonder who gave Tim this. What a douchebag. Maybe he had it before I met him and didn't know it. Yeah, that's probably it. Did he have sex with anyone while he was in California? What did I do to drive him away? Is he sleeping with anyone else here?* Jenae's head was spinning.

Two plastic grocery bags hung on each side of the 12-speed circular handlebars. This was the first time Jenae had allowed herself to splurge on comfort food since she had arrived in Hawaii. Nothing too crazy though: Fig Newton cookies, caramel-flavored rice cakes, and a carton of POG filled one bag and a pint of orange sherbet, cans of tuna packed in water, and two boxes of Wheat Thins filled the other. She really craved chocolate, but it was out of the question because it would've melted on the hot journey home. She had carefully placed her new medications into her fanny pack and rode out of the grocery store parking lot.

As she entered a busy intersection during rush hour, a vehicle turning right hit her and threw her onto the hot pavement. The bike slid underneath, behind the right front wheel of the car (thankfully not a bus), and Jenae's reflexes took over as she pulled the bike out of the path of the rear wheel. Her bags of groceries fell against the curb and Jenae was able to yank her and the 12-speed onto the sidewalk next to the road. She looked like a gymnast performing a floor routine, swiftly maneuvering jumps and lunges as if she had practiced it on mats in a gym in preparation for a big meet. The car didn't slow down or even stop, but a passenger looked back out of the window, leaning on the door with eyes as big as saucers. Jenae took shaky breaths while she leaned against a street sign pole. She surveyed her surroundings to make sure she was in a safe location as a car pulled up next to her and asked if she was all right. She waved them off, then looked down to see she had a gashed right knee and skinned shin. The 12-speed had a similar scrape down its body that scratched off a layer of light blue paint. Blood slowly seeped up through her excoriated skin and dripped down her leg, coating the imbedded road gravel in her ankle.

Jenae's eyes filled with tears as she got up to a standing position. Her bicycle was mostly intact, and the wheels were straight; she just had to adjust the brake pads, so they worked properly. The tape on the handlebars was tattered, but wouldn't be hard to fix. She leaned the bike against the signpost and reattached her grocery bags to the ram horn handles. Her mind was hyper-focused on her surroundings during the ride home, but when she shakily arrived at the Kaipuna parking garage, her tears began to flow, this time with a full-fledged guttural cry and abdominal heaving. Jenae's vulnerability was on full display, but no one was around to witness it, or to protect her from what was about to come her way.

Chapter 13

Betrayal

Jenae managed to compose herself and made it up the elevator to her apartment with bags in tow. She sat on the side of the tub with reddened eyes as she splashed lukewarm water gently on her wounds. She lathered up a soap bar and worked out the gravel bits that had gotten stuck in her leg.

"Hey Tim, I was wondering if we could chat after you get home from work tonight. I have something for you." Jenae left a message on his answering machine.

Walker picked up the phone before Jenae had a chance to hang up. "Hey Jenae, I just heard your message on speaker. Tim will be out until after dinner."

"Oh, hi, Walker. He isn't taking you to dinner, too?"

"No, I don't know what Tim's up to. I think he may be with Hannah and her friends tonight."

"Interesting. Can you have him call me when he gets home?"

"Sure, he should be around tomorrow if he doesn't get home at a decent hour to call you tonight."

"Thanks, Walker. See you later."

"Sure thing, Jenae. Have a good night."

———◆———

Jenae finally had a good night's sleep with the help of the sleeping pill that the doctor had prescribed. She could have slept until noon, but heard knocking at 10 AM. She rolled out of bed and spied through the peephole to see Tim looking side-to-side while waiting for her to open the door.

"Good morning; did I wake you up?" Tim remarked as she opened the door. "Geez, what happened to your leg? It's all torn up."

"I got hit by a car on my bike last night."

"Are you OK?"

"I think so. I noticed my helmet was cracked, but at least it wasn't my skull."

"Sorry you're hurt. Did the cops come?"

"No, nobody really noticed."

"Hopefully, you'll heal up before the triathlon."

"I should be fine in a few weeks, but training will be on hold for a while. I guess I can bike still – the 12-speed didn't get too banged up."

"I heard your message on the machine. You have something for me?"

Jenae's stomach dropped and her shoulders slumped as she sluggishly walked to her bedroom to retrieve the orange bottle of antibiotics for him. She held the bottle behind her back as she explained.

"I went to the doctor yesterday after work to get checked out. It turns out that I have chlamydia, which means you probably do, too."

Jenae handed him the bottle of pills as Tim's face twisted. He crossed his arms and thrust his chin up.

"What's this?"

"Antibiotics that you need to take for a week to get rid of it."

"How do you know that I have it?"

"Because you gave it to me! It is a sexually transmitted disease."

"I did not give it to you, because I don't have it."

"I'm pretty sure you did, Tim."

"The doctor gave me this prescription for my partner. He said that guys don't notice the infection like women do."

"How many bottles of medicine did you get, Jenae?"

"Are you kidding me? What do you mean... how many guys am I sleeping with? It's just you, Tim. How dare you? How'd you get the STD? Are you sleeping with other girls behind my back?"

"You're ridiculous. I gotta go." Tim let the door close hard behind him as he walked down the hallway back to his apartment with the bottle of pills in hand.

Jenae laid face down on her bed and cried into her pillow until the numbness of sleep replaced her consciousness of despair.

She wouldn't tell anyone else that she and Tim were treated for an STD, not even her best friend, Pami. The embarrassment was too much to face, especially because Pami was never keen on her and Tim being together. Jenae called in sick to the hospital for a few days to allow her leg injuries to heal, but more importantly, for her to pause her emotions and allow her heart to repair as well.

Pami had checked on her after the bike crash, but as far as Jenae knew, Pami didn't know that Jenae and Tim's relationship had gone awry. The next morning, Jenae found a handwritten note from Pami slipped under her door.

Dear Jenae, You are bigger than this, and you'll come out stronger on the other side.
Sometimes, the things that seem to hurt us most are the things that bring out the best in us.
Our struggles can help us discover the faith and strength we didn't know we had.
Challenges help us to see who we really are. And remember, we are here to

have FUN! Feel Better,
that's an order. I'm always
here if you need me. Love,
Pami

Jenae was grateful for at least one good friend from home.

Chapter 14

Gremmie

As Jenae lay in bed, memories of her sweet dog, Gremlin, came to her. She longed to have the comfort of Gremlin's little warm body next to her to soothe her pain. She missed her little doggy so much. Jenae's overly friendly Toto terrier was the best thing that came out of her previous relationship with her boyfriend in San Antonio. Well, Gremlin and late-night pizzas that Dean brought her after closing his Domino's store every night. Pepperoni, mushroom, and sausage won her heart and packed on fifteen pounds in no time. Her memories were vivid.

"Come on, Jenae, let's just look at dogs at the pound. It will be fun and we'll definitely not adopt a dog," Dean said.

While touring the dog kennels, Dean found a forever friend.

"Hey buddy, you look just like Gizmo with your ears poked straight out. Jenae, come meet Gizmo. Well, actually the card says her name is Ding-A-Ling. That's horrible. This dog must have been from an abusive home if they gave this sweet dog a

name like that. We could name her Gizmo, you know, like the good gremlin in the movie."

"I never saw that dumb movie and I don't think a dog is a good idea right now. You hang out at my place almost all the time, not to mention you're having surgery soon. That's a lot of pressure on me."

"But it'll be good for me to have a furry friend to hang out with for my recovery." Gremlin sat in Dean's lap and hung her head out of the window blowing her perfect gremlin ears in the wind as Jenae drove all three of them back to her apartment.

———◦◦◦———

Jenae claimed Gremlin as her own after Dean moved back to England with his family to fully recover from his surgery. "I'll be back in a few months, my love. I hope you'll wait for me." Dean professed on an overseas phone call. "I'm moving to Dallas, Dean. I think this is a good time to say goodbye...permanently," Jenae said with relief. Distance made the breakup so much easier. Jenae knew in her heart that Dean could never be a good partner for her because of his congenital kidney disease. She wanted true love, which she didn't have with Dean. More importantly, she didn't want her future children to have the risk of being born with the same dreadful disease. It sounds so cold and un-empathetic, but having healthy children with a strong, loving, and protective husband was the ultimate goal for Jenae.

Dean's goal was to marry a nurse who could take care of all of his needs.

————◆————

Gremlin hardly noticed that Dean was gone and settled into her two-bedroom Dallas apartment with her mistress just fine. She found an escape route off the patio most mornings when she was bored while Jenae slept in from her evening shifts at the medical center. Jenae was a neglectful pet owner by most standards because of her nonchalance about her dog's whereabouts. Gremlin often chased the big yellow tabby cat across the courtyard, which resulted in a hiss and a whack against her face by a cat's paw perched on a ledge above. "Gremlin! Gremlin! Where are you?" Jenae called with a gravelly morning voice. A few seconds later, a strange neighbor's door opened around the corner and Gremlin ran out down the sidewalk past Jenae, straight into her air-conditioned apartment. What the heck? Early the next morning, Jenae stealthily let Gremlin out to potty and watched from behind a porch plant. Gremlin trotted up to that same apartment that she was seen leaving the day before and scratched on the door. "Good morning, Gremlin!" A kind female voice came from the dark entrance as Gremlin eagerly ran inside and the door quickly shut behind her. Has Gremlin adopted another family? I think I heard little kids in there, Jenae thought as she dove back under her bed covers to finish out her sleep.

Gremlin's mysterious morning family stopped by a few months later to say "goodbye" to Gremlin. Jenae had never formally met them, but they were friendly. It was a strange revelation that Gremlin had foster parents without her knowledge.

With tears in her eyes, the mom said, "If you ever want to re-home Gremlin, here's our new number. We bought a house close by and we have a fenced backyard. We love her and would adopt her in a minute."

Jenae snapped herself out of her reminiscing daydream, and in a deep state of guilt, she called her mom to check on Gremlin.

"She's fine, Jenae. She's made friends with all the neighbors and loves chasing squirrels up the trees. I'll see you next month. We can't wait to visit."

After a few days of hanging out in her condo in isolation and self-reflection, Jenae reappeared in public early one evening. She had rested enough to ride her bike to the Jack in the Box for a coveted chicken fajita pita and even splurged with a side of guacamole added to the order. She headed to the beach, sat in the long shade of a tall wooden lifeguard stand, and savored her pita sandwich while slurping down an extra large Diet Coke with extra ice. She delicately touched the skin around her leg wounds, inspecting them for signs of infection while being careful not to introduce sand into them. Most of the abrasions were starting to scab over, but they were not healed enough for her to bathe in the ocean.

In the shadow of the setting sun, Sand Jesus suddenly appeared at her side, startling Jenae. Her eyes blinked rapidly while she discerned whether it was really a man or a mirage. When she was certain he was incarnate, she gave the bronzed man with long blonde hair a quick hand gesture and said, "Hi," with a nervous smile. He looked at her with his steely blue eyes, extended his arms by his side, smiled and nodded her way as he sauntered behind her and continued down the beach without saying a word.

Maybe that's a sign I should go back to church on Sundays, Jenae thought as she felt peace in her heart and uneasiness in her gut.

Two days off of work was long enough; any longer, and Jenae would have needed a doctor's note stating that she could return. *Ain't nobody got time for that,* Jenae chuckled to herself. When she returned to her condo, she realized that she was out of contact solution for the next day. She reluctantly called Tim to borrow from his supply. Walker answered the phone.

"Sure, you can borrow some. I'm sure Tim wouldn't mind. He isn't here right now, though, and I'm headed out the door to go on a date. Come by in the morning, and I'll give it to you then."

Before work early the next morning, Jenae knocked on Tim's door. Nobody answered immediately. She knocked again and waited.

She heard, "Who is it?" yelled from inside.

"It's Jenae! I came to borrow some contact solution." Tim opened the door slightly with the chain still attached.

"Walker said I could borrow some of your contact solution before I go to work."

"Oh, he didn't tell me. He didn't come home last night. I'll go get some for you." Tim left the door chained while he retrieved a bottle of saline for Jenae. He handed it to her through the impenetrable doorway.

"What is going on? Why didn't you let me in?" Jenae squinted and furrowed her forehead.

Tim scratched his face, looking up at Jenae with his chin tucked.

"Um, I have somebody in here with me."

Jenae's chest tightened, and her face turned red. Then she heard a familiar voice.

"Who is at the door, Teeim?"

Jenae could feel all of her blood plummet down into her legs. She felt like puking as she walked away slowly, not uttering another word.

Chapter 15

Rock Bottom

"Let me in!" Walker pounded on Jenae's door after she returned home from a welcomed distracting 10-hour work shift.

"I need to explain something to you," Walker squawked desperately.

As Walker sat down on the couch, he spouted all the reasons why Tim did what he did.

"Listen, Tim was really upset about the whole medication thing. He thought you'd been messing around on him."

"I don't believe you, Walker – he's been the slutty one. I know I didn't give it to him. And now I find him in bed with Hannah? How long has this been going on?"

"Well, that isn't for me to explain. But I can tell you that my mama has had conversations with Tim lately, asking him why he hadn't been dating Hannah. Her mama and our mama have been conspiring for them to get together. I think Tim just finally gave in to it."

"What happened to Hannah's boyfriend, Ronin?"

"They broke up, I guess. That's why she came prowling around Tim. To be honest, I think Tim is tired of Hannah already, because she does get around a lot."

"That isn't a secret to anyone. I'm not speaking to Tim or Hannah anymore. They're both dead to me."

"Isn't that going to be difficult with Hannah as your roommate?"

"Not anymore; she'll have the place to herself. Pami offered me to stay in the empty room in her apartment. I don't care if I ever see either of them again in my life."

"Hold on, you're still going to do the triathlon with Tim in a few weeks, right?"

"Hail no! He can do it by himself. Seriously, I don't ever want to see his lying, cheating face again. He disgusts me."

"Well, Tim isn't going to like to hear that. Please do the triathlon. You don't have to talk to him or even look at him. I'll make him ride in the back of the truck on the way over to Kaneohe. You can ride in the cab with me."

"Why do you even care, Walker?" Jenae's eyes were filled with tears.

"Because you've been such a good influence in Tim's life this summer. He's fitter and more health conscience, and you know that he worries about his cholesterol and dying at a young age like our dad and grandpa did."

Jenae looked down with her chin propped on her fist. In a monotone voice, she replied, "I'll think about it. Only if I don't have to speak to him and my leg wounds are healed up by then."

"Oh shuga, those wounds look painful. I bet you will be 100% in a few weeks."

"We'll see." Jenae opened the door for Walker as he strode into the hallway.

———◆———

Work was Jenae's priority for the next few weeks. She wanted to focus solely on her patients, but the stress she was feeling put her in her head most of the day. She was never hungry because her stomach was doing somersaults throughout her shift. She barely got the vitamin C wafers chewed up before her ride to work in the morning. When she sat in front of the chef salad that she bought from the cafeteria for lunch, she could only eat a few bites before she surrendered to laying her head on the table next to the pile of greens. Tears seeped out of her closed eyes as she wondered if she should give in to the profound hopelessness she was feeling. Everything in her body hurt, and she wanted the pain to stop.

She was too embarrassed to talk to Pami about how bad it had gotten. Pami knew that Hannah was pleased about breaking Tim and Jenae up, but was taken aback by Hannah's *schadenfreude.* Hannah got pleasure from Jenae's pain.

During an afternoon of working while half asleep, Jenae joined the post-op transport team to move her new patient from the gurney to the bed.

"OK, lift on three. One, two, three," said the transporter. All at once, five people surrounding the patient lifted and yanked him to his bed in one fell swoop. On Jenae's side, a drain tube from the wound site got stuck in the gurney and pulled out of the patient in the hasty transfer. As the tube and bulb swung from the side of the rolling bed, Jenae heard her nurse manager behind her. "This is your fault, Jenae. You should have cleared the tubing before he moved." Jenae hadn't even noticed that a drain was on her side because it was wrapped in heating blankets. Her confidence sunk even lower.

She found herself tearing up in waves of emotion as she called the surgeon to inform him of her mistake. He was surprisingly kind to her. "I think it will be alright. I put extra drains in, and some of them weren't sutured in place." Jenae still felt like a failure.

On break, she went to the outdoor pay phone near the café. As she pulled out her long-distance calling card, she plugged in the 10-digit number to reach her oldest brother for support and to pull her off the proverbial edge of despondency. As luck would have it, his secretary put her right through to his phone.

"I'm just really sad and tired," Jenae squeaked as she cried with tears streaming down her cheeks." She couldn't tell him about the betrayal and breakup because that would sound stupid.

"Are you sleeping and eating these days?" her brother asked.

"I'm training for a triathlon, and I got hit by a car. I have injuries from that."

"Are you OK? Did they take x-rays?"

"No, it really wasn't that big of a deal. I just have some abrasions and bruising. They should heal in time for the event, but I can't fully train right now."

"Maybe you can take a leisurely bike ride on your day off. Just enjoy yourself. You don't have to push it too hard."

"Yeah, I can do that."

"And what are you eating?"

"I'm really not hungry. My appetite is gone because I'm stressed out. I've been trying to eat healthy and reduce calories."

"It sounds like you need to pick up some fruits and vegetables and some protein, like a chicken from the deli, on the way home from work. Have something in your apartment that you can grab when you're hungry."

"OK, I can do that, too."

"Are you going to be alright? I have a meeting in a few minutes. You can call me anytime if you are feeling bad."

"Yeah, thanks for talking to me. Love you."

"Love you too, Jenae."

Her eldest brother loved to rescue everyone, all of his younger siblings, his multiple girlfriends, and his mother, but he never rescued a pet. He hated dogs. He was the go-to-guy in a crisis. He made Jenae feel like she could persevere in the face of adversity.

Common sense advice and support from her protective eldest brother turned Jenae around from feeling like a blubbering victim to a wounded warrior willing to fight another day. Her confidence took more time, but Jenae felt that she was back on track. Her heart was only partially broken now.

———◆———

With a refrigerator full of fresh, healthy food, Jenae cooked herself a chicken and vegetable stir-fry without the eggs for one last meal in the apartment that she shared with Hannah. Jenae had plans to officially move into the empty bedroom in Pami's apartment and completely erase her friendship with Hannah and Tim. She treated herself with dessert to celebrate: mango, pineapple, and papaya smothered in layers of whipped cream. *Just one or two more rounds around the bowl will do. Shwerrr, Shwerrr, Shwerrr, Shwerrr.* She loved the sound of whipped cream being sprayed out of the can.

As Jenae finished her bedtime routine, the phone rang. Jenae ambled to the living room in her pajamas and a towel on her head to answer it. *This is the first time I've heard this phone ring; it's probably the wrong number, or maybe it is from somebody at the front door trying to get in.*

"Hi, is Hannah there?"

"Uh, no; she isn't. Can I take a message?"

"This is Ronin. I was hoping to talk to her in person."

"Are you calling from the front of the building?"

"Actually, I am."

"She isn't here. Do you want to leave a note for her?"

"Can I come up and write it there?"

"Sure, I'll buzz you in. Do you know where the apartment is?"

"Oh yeah, I'm there with Hannah almost every day while you are at work."

"Ah, good to know."

Ronin appeared different than Jenae had remembered him at the start of the summer. His face was pale, and his eyes were reddened and puffy. He did seem comfortable when he plopped down on the couch as if he owned the place.

"Alright then, I'll find a pen and a piece of paper."

"I really thought Hannah would be here. Did she say where she was going?"

"Ronin, I've barely seen her, and I know very little about her comings and goings."

Ronin leaned forward with his elbows on his knees and held his face in the palms of his hands.

"Are you alright?" Jenae asked.

"We had a fight, and I haven't slept in days. She won't talk to me."

"I'm sorry about that. Maybe you two can work it out."

"You think so?"

"I don't know, maybe."

Ronin finished his note and carefully placed it on Hannah's bed.

"I'm supposed to go to work tonight, but I've got the worst migraine. Do you have any aspirin or Tylenol that I could take?"

"Sure, let me see what I've got." Jenae retreated to her bedroom suite and found different kinds of pills in her bedside table drawer, including a sleeping pill that she was planning to take before bed. "I've got some chewable vitamin C. That should help get rid of a migraine."

"No thanks, just a couple of Tylenol's will do."

"Here, I have these in a blister packet. I think they're samples."

"Thanks, I'm just going to go home and try to sleep it off. I wouldn't be of any value at work tonight, anyway."

"Ok, goodnight. I hope everything works out."

Chapter 16

Patient Advice

The next day at work, Jenae took morning report on her patients. Duke was a 49-year-old black male who returned from a surgical debridement of his left foot the evening before. He was on IV antibiotics and had orders for dressing changes twice a day and blood sugar checks before each meal and before bed. A medical description of a patient and doctor's orders created a checklist of nursing duties that were required during each shift. Additionally, a full assessment of the patient with vital signs was done at the beginning of each shift. After listening to the patient's lungs, heart and abdomen, Jenae palpated for abdominal distention and touched the arms and legs to assess for fluid retention and capillary flow in the toenail beds. She checked his IV site and dressings for drainage or bleeding. Jenae checked pulses and strength in the upper and lower extremities as she talked to the patient about his pain level, bowel movements, and checked his urinary output in the catheter bag hung on the side of the bed. A nurse's job starts with physical needs of a patient and progresses into emotional support and education to help facilitate complete healing.

Duke was on a work-recruiting trip to the Hawaiian Islands for the Texas Rangers. There were two baseball players that he had an eye on and made the journey from LA for a week work/vacation. The first night on Waikiki, he stepped on a sharp object in the sand and sliced his foot open. He ignored the cut for five days until the skin turned flaming red and pus was draining from the wound. When the foot was too painful to put weight on it, he visited the Queen's hospital emergency department and was admitted. It may have healed on its own with early proper wound care, but diabetes and peripheral neuropathy threw a wrench into the equation and he needed immediate care to ward off a potential amputation.

"I really need to get out of here and back to LA this week for my daughter's wedding activities," Duke said with a grimace as he tried to readjust his leg in the bed.

"Here, let me help you get comfortable. Let's put this pillow under your knee and elevate that foot. Is that better?" Jenae gently lifted his leg into position and raised the head of his bed as she fluffed his pillow behind him and released the sheet from his toes.

"It's more comfortable, but I'll probably need a pain med when it is time."

"Sure, I'll bring it in with your next antibiotic. My notes say you can have something in 30 minutes. So when is the wedding? Is she your first to get married?"

"She's my oldest and only daughter, so it's kind of emotional for dear old dad. Time just flew by, and soon she'll start her own family. The actual ceremony is next month, but she wants help from her mom and me with the last-minute details, and the checks to cover the cost of the festivities, of course. Are you married?"

"Not yet, but hopefully I'll find the right guy soon. You know the phrase, always a bridesmaid and never a bride?"

"Of course."

"That's me. I have five bridesmaid dresses hanging in a special closet in my parents' house to remind me. One is a brown Little House on the Prairie dress with lace. Then there's a royal blue satin dress and a black satin dress. A sea foam satin dress probably complimented my complexion the best, and the latest addition was a mauve, lacy, number that I wore for my sister's wedding a couple of months ago."

"Wow, that's impressive. I have no idea what my daughter's bride's maids will be wearing, but I heard it is an important decision."

"It's fun wearing a beautiful dress for the day. It's too bad they'll never be worn again. I just got a letter from my dear friend who lives in West Virginia now asking if I'd be in her wedding in six weeks."

"What kind of dress do you think she'll pick out for you?"

"I wish I could be there for her, but I can't go because I'm working here and the distance is too far to travel for one weekend. I can't wait to see the pictures, though."

"Our family and most of my daughter's friends are local, so we're lucky we've got that in our favor. My future son-in-law is a great guy, and he has an impressive friend group who are high achievers. They should be happy together. My fatherly advice is to never settle for less than you deserve. The right guy will come along when God wills it."

"It sounds like you are going to have a wonderful celebration. Let me go get your meds and I'll be back in a flash."

Jenae tried to never miss an opportunity to learn from her patients and this time she gained a little more perspective on what was important in relationships, which gave her hope of finding that right guy with a supportive family.

Work had gotten easier for Jenae, and she felt like she was part of the team.

"Do you want to meet at Hanauma Bay for some morning snorkeling this weekend? Some of us from work are planning a little excursion," Rhonda asked Jenae with a smile and eyebrow raises.

"Sure, I love to snorkel. How early should we get there?"

"Let's plan on nine-thirty at the latest to avoid the major crowds," Rhonda recommended.

"OK, I'll ride my bike there from Waikiki. You know I have the triathlon next week and my training has been lacking, to say the least. Is it OK if I meet all of you there?"

"Of course, but if you arrive first, be sure to wait for us."

Saturday morning rolled around and normally Jenae felt put out by having another social event, but this time she looked forward to time with her work mates outside of the hospital and away from Waikiki. In addition to two grams of chewable vitamin C, Jenae prepared herself a piece of toast with peanut butter and sliced mango. She filled both of her water bottles with ice and water, and slipped on her two-piece turquoise and black dive swimming suit. She grabbed her goggles and snorkel on the way out and walked through the hallways of the Kaipuna with her clip-on bike shoes. *Clip, clop, clip, clop.*

As she rode down the empty streets of the Ala Wai Canal, a cool morning mist fogged her shield style sunglasses. Jenae had splurged on sporty reflective glasses when she picked up a new helmet at the bike shop earlier in the week.

Part of the ride to Hanauma Bay was on next week's triathlon route. Jenae wanted to practice the long hill climb leading up to the bay because it would be halfway in the cycle leg of the triathlon and an especially grueling trial. But before challenging the hill, she meandered through the streets of Honolulu, through Kapiolani Park on Paki Drive, past Coconut Avenue to the ocean side of Diamond Head. She saw a large group of surfers hanging loose on their boards and catching medium sized waves in the turquoise waterscape. After picking up speed on the shoulder of the H1 highway, Jenae smiled when she caught a first glimpse of the jet-ski platform floating offshore from Hawaii Kai. A red light on the freeway intersection allowed her to grab a bottle of water from its holder and take a few chugs once she pulled the plastic nipple cover out with her front teeth. The ride up the hill made her chest burn, and she could taste blood from tiny capillaries breaking loose in her lungs from the strain of the incline. *This is going to be rougher next week after the swim, with a longer bike ride from up north.* Jenae questioned her abilities.

Reaching the top of the hill represented a small victory for the morning as Jenae coasted down the winding path, tapping her hand brakes strategically as she glided into the beach area of Hanauma Bay. She locked her bike up to a post; she leaned against it with her palms as she stretched her legs behind her. Her calves and hamstrings needed an extra release after the grind up the hill.

Jenae arrived earlier than expected, which gave her time to cool off in the ocean before her friends' arrival. It also gave her reddened face a chance to return to a normal shade. With competition goggles and a loosely attached snorkel, she easily swam around the outskirts of the rock formations to the coral reefs. She gently rotated each arm as she took relaxed side breaths and flutter kicked without a splash. In her mind, she was preparing her body to peak for the race; like she had done so many times before in her competitive swimming career.

As the waves pushed Jenae off of the reef, she swooshed by a juvenile turtle and a school of yellow clown fish. The sand blew off the bottom of the ocean, lowering visibility that gave concealment to sea creatures from human spectators floating above.

Cool tap water from the beachside shower rained down on Jenae's face and head as she first placed her hand into the stream and then her arm. She rotated to feel the coolness on her sun kissed shoulders and back. As she opened her eyes and wiped her face, she saw three very short, black-haired, middle-aged women observing her from an uncomfortably close-proximity. They smiled and waved at her in their loose-fitting garments and big floppy hats. They acted as if she had met them before. *Was one of them a patient of mine at the hospital?* In Dallas she occasionally ran into patients outside of the hospital setting, like in line at the grocery store, who had given her that same glance.

"Hi," one woman said timidly, with a grin.

"Hello," Jenae gave a half wave.

In broken English, the bravest woman had a request. "We from Japan. We take picture, you?"

Jenae ran her hands in her hair to ring out the excess water.

"You want me to take your picture?" Jenae dried her hands on the towel and reached out for their camera. The Japanese ladies giggled as they turned heads and looked at each other, covering their mouths with their dainty, pale hands.

"No, no. We take picture with you."

"With me?" Jenae said, confused.

"Yes, we take picture together."

"OK." Jenae shrugged.

The ladies squealed in delight and looked behind them and waved toward their group for the other ladies to join them. The rest of the group had waited and watched while their scouts secured a picture with a tall American.

"You so BIG!"

"And pretty. Movie Star?"

"No, No. I am just a regular woman."

Jenae towered over the squadron of tourists in her sporty bikini and gave the shaka hand sign and a bright smile with each camera click.

She grabbed her disposable underwater camera from her fanny pack and advanced the film.

"Ok, now I want a picture of all of you with me." She handed the camera to a random guy drying off from the shower. "Everybody say *Cheese.*"

It was an odd moment from a group of strangers that gave Jenae a boost of confidence that she desperately needed.

Rhonda and her nurse-friends hiked down the roadway, and waved as they approached the beach with Jenae in their sights.

"We had to park so far away. Sorry we are a little bit late."

"No problem, I was just having a photo shoot with my new friends."

Chapter 17

The Big Race

Confidence was not in Jenae's psyche on the day of the race, and Tim was nowhere to be found as she met Walker in the parking garage with a big beach bag full of essentials.

"Do you have all of your race stuff, Jenae? Your water bottles, snacks, your race packet with your bib number, ankle monitor, and swim cap?"

"I hope so, Manager Walker. I love my new long-sleeved triathlon shirt that came in the race packet. Thanks for keeping us organized."

"What else are you forgetting: your helmet, sunglasses, sunscreen, bike cleats, extra socks, running shoes, bike shorts, running shorts, goggles? Don't forget your goggles!"

"You're more nervous about this race than me."

"Somehow I feel responsible for y'all's success."

"I put your bike in the back of the truck. I'll run upstairs, find Tim, and get his bike loaded up too."

"Let me guess, he's entertaining an overnight guest again."

"No silly, it's game day! I told him to wait in the apartment until I gave him the all clear because he knows you don't want to talk to him."

"Very clever, but that's stupid, Walker. I'm going to end up saying at least a few words to him today."

"I know, but I promised you that he'd ride in the back of the truck to the event and he agreed to it. I just think it is funny that he'll be back there with his hair whipping in the wind like a dog."

"Thanks for having my back, Walker."

Tim emerged from the metal stairwell door wearing red latex swim trunks, a gray singlet cotton shirt, and flip-flops on his feet. He carried a big military duffle bag over his left shoulder as he gave Jenae a sheepish smile and said, "Hello."

"Hey." It was the first word Jenae had spoken to Tim since the contact solution incident. She still hadn't looked Hannah in the eyes – much less talked to her, which was doable since Jenae had moved in with Pami.

"I guess I'm riding in the back of the truck."

"Yep."

"Sure are brother."

Tim was willing to serve his penance when it related to Jenae. He still had strong feelings for her and wouldn't stop trying to get her back. The likelihood that he had given Jenae the STD was high because he had hooked up with a party girl while training in California. But he would never admit that to Jenae. Tim felt doubly bad for hooking up with Hannah because it hurt Jenae so badly, but also because Tim later realized that Hannah was using him. He sat on his duffel bag against the back of the cab and looked through the window to try to figure out what Walker and Jenae were laughing about.

Walker maneuvered the big red truck close to the triathlon bike transition area set up in a parking lot near the start of the race. Jenae rolled her bike with one hand to a center slot and prepped her area. She placed her mid-calf socks into her bike shoes and neatly set a beach towel on top. Her new helmet, with her shades stuck inside, was clipped to the 12-speed's crossbar, and two full water bottles were squeezed into the wire racks. Running shoes and extra socks remained in the bag along with a carbohydrate-refueling bar that she picked up at the bike shop. Tim repeated the setup for his equipment one rack over, out of Jenae's line of sight.

"All registered racers come to the official's tent for confirmation and to get numbers marked on your arm and leg," said a booming voice over a loud-speaker. Tim had picked up both of their race packets at the base a few days before, which allowed them to figure out the placement of the bib numbers and the electronic ankle sensor ahead of time. They stood in line outside the tent and waited their turn to be marked up with black grease pencils.

"Are you ready for this?" Tim asked Jenae.

"Not really, are you?"

"Probably not, but I've had a few weeks of good workouts leading up to today. I think I lost a few pounds."

"Good for you. The bike wreck messed me up on training, so I'm not expecting much."

"Promise me you won't give up, Jenae. You have to finish the whole race, OK?"

"I'll do my best."

"I gave Walker my good camera, so he is going to be taking pictures of us along the route."

They reached separate tables at the same time.

"It feels official now that we're marked. What's your race number?" Jenae asked.

"I'm 250. You're 252. Huh, I wonder who got in between us?" Tim said.

"No comment," Jenae replied.

Professional male racers were summoned to the front of the group for the first wave of the swim. *Beep, Beep, Beep.* The starting signal sounded. The triathlon had officially begun. Professional women lined up right behind the men and started two minutes later in a second wave to prevent them from drafting off of the group ahead. Forty men identified by the letter A before their numbers and twenty-five women identified by the letter B before their numbers were there to compete for big prize money. Four hundred more amateur participants, including Tim and Jenae, filled out the field of racers. Half of the amateurs were competing on a team of three. Each team member did one leg of the race. Although Jenae had asked Tim if he wanted to do the team approach earlier in the summer, he poo-pooed it with a comment about not wanting to be a weakling.

"OK, see the two big orange inflated buoys out there?" Tim pointed out to the bay covered in low-lying clouds.

"Yeah, do we go around them clockwise or counterclockwise?"

"Go to the left one first. It is 625 meters out. Take a right turn around the buoy and beeline it to the other one, which is about 250 meters. Make another right turn around the outside of that buoy and book it into shore another 625 meters. I think that is 1.5 kilometers."

"That shouldn't be too tough. I'm wondering the best strategy for getting out of the water with the beach and waves."

"I'm going to swim in as far as possible before standing up and running to the transition area," Tim said.

"Good plan. I think they're calling for the amateur men's group now. That's you!"

"Alright, I'll see you on the other side."

"Good luck!"

Tim slipped on his goggles and lined up in a mass huddle hip-deep in the water with other male competitors wearing rubber ducky yellow swim caps. The front of the group walked forward and lay down in the water when it reached their chests and churned their arms fast and furiously, creating an unremitting splash zone. Most swimmers were clumped together on the shortest vector headed for the first orange buoy. Others opted for a less aggressive approach and gave a wide berth to the crowd.

"Get down there, Jenae! I promised Tim I would get some good pictures. Don't miss your start time." Walker stood to the side of the starting line in a hoodie slicker and a baseball cap to keep warm in the early morning light rain shower.

"Women amateurs, get on the line." *Beep, Beep, Beep...* "And the final wave is off and headed for the first buoy," the starting official announced on the loudspeaker.

Jenae couldn't stop her competitive fever when she hit the water with a half dive off of the sand bottom. Her strategy was to get ahead of the pack and stay ahead to avoid the assault of arms flying ubiquitously. She wasn't so lucky at first and ended up locked in between two women; she was elbowed from one side, then the other. She elbowed back a few times and made a path to the front of the pack, which allowed her to avoid flutter-kick turbulence. Swimmers lifted their yellow-capped heads to spy the direction of the first turn. Officials were waiting on small boats and surfboards to watch for disqualifications by cutting the course short and to make sure nobody drowned or got taken out to sea by a shark.

Professional racers hit the beach and mounted their bikes before Jenae reached the second buoy. Tim wasn't too far ahead of her, and she wanted to catch him to teach him a lesson and maybe humiliate him a little bit too.

Jenae's finish to the beach was easier than expected because there were no big waves to navigate as she pulled off her swim cap and ran to her bike nearby. She'd passed a few male swimmers on the way in, and on the loudspeaker, she heard her name.

"Jenae from Dallas, Texas, is our first finisher for the amateur woman on the first leg of the race."

"Where did she come from? I don't see her name on previous rosters," the announcers bantered.

"We'll have to keep an eye on her throughout the race."

Then she heard a familiar voice cheering for her in the distance. It was Walker.

"You're in first place, Jenae! Keep it up!"

A little embarrassed, Jenae thought, *if they only knew how dreadful I am at cycling and running. They'll find out soon enough.* Jenae waved to Walker. "Thanks!"

"You almost beat Tim; he is still getting on his bike."

Tim waved as Jenae looked in his direction. He strolled his bike to the edge of the transition station and ate a goop packet for energy as Jenae caught up to him.

"Great job on the swim," Tim told Jenae.

"Thanks, you too. I think you'll beat me in the next two legs, though. Go on ahead. I'll meet you at the finish line."

Tim stood up on his bike pedals to get momentum and sped off to catch the men in the pack ahead. "See ya later!"

Some road bikes in the race were super fancy. It was the first time Jenae had seen bikes with discs on the rear wheels. *Those must belong to the professional athletes.* Carbon fiber technology was new to the sport and very expensive for average athletes. They cost at least ten times the amount Jenae and Tim spent on their bikes from the local Schwinn outlet. Tim wore long latex shorts that morphed from a swimsuit to bike shorts seamlessly. Jenae wore a similar ensemble of a sturdy workout bra and bike shorts. They only needed to slip on their socks and bike shoes and clip the bike helmet under their chins at the transition. The professional women wore one-piece speedo swimsuits on the swim and the ride. Professional men only wore a tiny speedo swimsuit, clip-in shoes, and a helmet on their heads. They had earned the right to compete almost naked because they had the finest, most balanced physiques of all athletes. Not an ounce of fat was on display.

As bikers moved inland, the clouds disappeared, and the hot sun made a relentless showing for the rest of the race. Temperatures spiked to the high 90s as racers made their way to the outskirts of Honolulu, where temperatures amplified in the concrete jungle. Jenae was on familiar turf now as she rode her usual training route on H1 to the east. She distracted her mind to endure the pain by recalling fun activities she had at memorable places as she passed by. She sang songs to herself to keep her cycle tempo up to at least 60 rpm. For some reason, the Queen song kept popping into her brain... *another one bites the dust....* On the flat stretches, she could lean into the handlebars on her forearms and duck her head for maximum efficiency. It was also a good position to hydrate from her two plastic bottles.

As she climbed the dreaded hill from Hawaii Kai to Hanauma Bay, she saw a big red truck parked across the freeway with a big, blonde-haired Walker hollering at her. "Smile! I'm taking your picture." Jenae growled back, "Walker, get over here and pick me up! I quit!" As Jenae continued up the incline – she passed a woman stopped on the shoulder, attempting to repair a flat tire on her bike. Walker drove the truck slowly next to Jenae, keeping pace with her, just long enough to roll down the window for a brief conversation.

"At least you don't have a flat tire like that lady back there."

"I'm exhausted, and I'm out of water, Walker. Put my bike in the back of the truck and drive me to the finish line."

"I can't do that, Jenae. Tim would kill me. But seriously, I wanted to warn you about the descent up here. The grade is steep and curvy, and it has sand on it. One of the professional guys wiped out on it and ripped his speedo, and his tiny ass was sticking out. An official gave him a big yellow sponge that he put in his suit to hide his butt. It looks funny as hell."

"All the more reason for you to rescue me from my hell!"

Walker sped off in the big red truck, not to be seen again by Jenae until the end of the bike ride.

Chapter 18

Finished

J enae's ride down the curvy hill next to the ocean was
less scary than anticipated. Sand that created a disaster
for the leading men had been swept aside, and race officials
were diligent about directing bikers around the dangerous
curve. For the first time on the bike leg of the race, Jenae felt
comfortable in the saddle. A cool breeze was blowing on shore,
which gave her a tailwind that she desperately needed.

Tim had made it to the finish of the 40K bike leg and
started the 10K run around the base. Walker drove Tim's red
truck to strategic pull-offs and parking lots to get glimpses
and photographic proof of Tim as he jogged by. Tim's stature
was strong, but stiff. He picked up every tiny cup of water or
Gatorade that was offered to him along the route and stopped
to touch his toes as he took sips of the blue-colored fluid. He'd
run out of water on the bike leg like most riders, and excessive
heat had caused more cases of dehydration than expected.

At 4 kilometers into the running route, he came upon
paramedics huddled over a racer lying down under a shade tree.

An emergency crew tended to the racer with cooling towels and inserted an IV before they carted him on a gurney into an ambulance parked on the side of the road. As Tim jogged closer to the patient, he recognized him as one of his Marine buddies in his training group.

"Oh shit! Where are they taking him?" Tim asked a race official.

"I assume he is going to Tripler Army Hospital."

"What happened? Did he pass out?"

"I'm not sure, but I'd guess heat stroke or something like that."

Tim slowed his pace to just above a power walk and gave up worrying about his race time. *I guess if I finish in these conditions I'll be satisfied.*

Tim and Walker sat near the transition area with ice-cold wet t-shirts over their heads when Jenae completed the bike ride. They watched her take off her helmet and bike shoes, and slowly reach for her running shoes and fresh socks. She told herself that she could do this; she was going to finish this race even though every muscle and bone in her body ached. Each leg lift to slip on her shoes was a painful effort. After wiping her beet-red face with a wet towel, she put on a sun visor and jogged toward the running route.

"Only 10K to go!" Walker hollered her way as she approached the brothers lounging in the shady grass on the side of the road.

"It's a hot, tough run, Jenae. You may want to bail out by the look of your red face," Tim said.

"I have to finish." Jenae might have cried if she had any tears left.

"Take it easy and drink a lot along the way. We won't be upset if you don't do the run, but we'll stay as long as it takes for you to finish."

Tim's quip hit Jenae on her last nerve. *What a jerk... we are willing to wait no matter how long it takes you, even though it might be midnight.* Her legs loosened up with each step, and she perked up as she approached the first hydration station on the route. Normally, runners swiftly grab a paper cup as they pass by and drink it or dump it over their head. Jenae stopped at the table, looked at each cup, and asked, "So, what are you serving today?" She grabbed an orange one and drank it as she threw her head back. Spots filled her vision field, and in an attempt to ward off a dizzy spell, Jenae tried to drink another cup but couldn't do it.

That was it, game over. Jenae dumped a few cups of water over her head; her body chilled immediately. She squeezed her eyes shut as she walked back to the transition area. Jenae stood before Tim with her hands on her hips and her head bowed. Tim slowly stood up and laid his hand on her back. "You did a great job." He was relieved to see her still vertical-not horizontal in an ambulance like his Marine buddy.

Walker drove the wounded warriors back to Waikiki with one stop at a local convenience store to pick up extra super-duper Gatorade fountain drinks. Tim was allowed to sit in the front cab of the truck again, but he and Jenae were speechless and too exhausted to communicate. They listened in a daze as Walker gave a play-by-play account of the entire race, including the best snack and drink tables.

"Hey, why don't you come hang out with us at my apartment to recuperate?" Tim unloaded Jenae's belongings and carried them into the building and onto the elevator for her.

"I don't know."

"Is Pami home? You should have help while you recover, just in case you blew a gasket back there."

"Pami's working today. Do you have any good food at your place?"

"I have tuna, dill pickles, and crackers. But I can have Walker go out and get anything we want to eat. Sushi, steak, burgers, aloha plate?"

"How about a chicken fajita pita with guacamole?" Jenae asked.

"Sure, I'll get a burger and fries. I think I earned it today."

"Hey Walker..."

Jenae took up half the couch with her legs slightly bent as she laid her head sideways on the back of the furniture. Her bucket of electrolyte soda was nuzzled between her legs. A guitar riff from a Guns N' Roses music video woke her up from her stupor long enough to take a few sips of her drink. Tim dried his hair with a towel after a quick shower and sat in a chair across the room. He picked up the phone receiver and dialed a number that he found in a phone book on the side table.

"Hey, how are you doing? What happened? Dude, you were pushing it too hard. How long are you going to be there? OK, call me if you need a ride back home."

"Who was that?"

"That was my Marine buddy. He ended up in the emergency room from the race."

"No way, what happened?"

"He was pushing it really hard trying to stay up with the professionals, and it sounds like he got heat stroke. They gave him a couple of bags of fluid already, but his heart rhythm still isn't right."

"Dang, that's scary. It was so friggin' hot on the course today."

"I didn't want to tell you about him until I knew he was alright."

"Did Walker know about this?"

"Yes, but he didn't want to scare you either. The extreme heat wave did a lot of people in."

"Including me," Jenae said with shame.

"I was so relieved when I saw you walking back because I was worried you'd collapse, too."

"Why didn't you just tell me before the run?"

"Because I knew if I told you to stop, your pigheadedness would kick in, and you'd continue on no matter what. It had to be solely your decision."

"Thanks for caring, I guess. I am disappointed in myself, but at least I'm not a patient in the hospital."

After eating lunch and staring at MTV for another few hours, Jenae made her way back to Pami's apartment. She sat in the bathtub and soaked until the water turned cold. When she got out of the tub, she lay on the bed with just a towel and said a prayer, *Thank you, Lord Jesus for getting me through today and all the difficult times I've had here. Thank you for protecting me, Tim, and all the racers in Your Golden Light today. Please send me clear signs of Your Will because I'm not making very good decisions on my own. And by the way, who exactly is Sand Jesus? Amen.*

Chapter 19

Parental Rights

"Aloha!" Jenae upgraded her ritual of greeting visitors in the baggage claim area at the HNL airport by purchasing fragrant live flower leis for both of her parents. She retired the everlasting Kukui nut necklaces that she had lying around her apartment.

"Hi! Thanks for picking us up." Jenae placed a lei around her mother's neck, rested it on her shoulders, and bent down to give her a kiss on the cheek.

"Welcome to Hawaii!" She did the same routine with her dad. He lifted the flowers to his nose for a sniff as she stood on her tiptoes to kiss his bearded cheek.

"Thank you, what a nice welcome."

"Absolutely. I'm glad you both could make it. The car is just over in the parking lot, so when you get your bags, follow me there."

"It's been so long since we have been to Hawaii. I think you were a little girl when your dad and I came for the first and last time. It was magical. I remember the whole island smelled of perfume from the flowers. Just like this lei."

"With any luck, you'll be able to make some more memories while you are here, Mom."

"I hope so. It's too bad that your dad is leaving to Japan for a conference in a couple of days."

"You could have joined me, dear."

"I think I'll have more fun spending the week with my daughter in Hawaii."

"Thanks, Mom; we should have a good time."

"Whose car are we using? I thought we'd have to take a cab."

"It belongs to a nurse friend of mine. She's very generous and lets us borrow it anytime."

"Well, tell her that we appreciate it very much." Jenae navigated traffic on the side streets of Honolulu while she pointed out places of interest to her parents. They eventually made it to the hotel.

"I want to go in with you when you check into the hotel. I made the reservation as a Kamaaina with my Hawaii driver's license, so I got you a better rate. The Royal Hawaiian can be very pricey, and I know that you wanted to stay in the original pink palace."

"Oh, yes! How exciting! We're really looking forward to this hotel stay. Listen to this, the brochure says:

> *The Royal Hawaiian was built in 1927. The iconic Royal Hawaiian, a Luxury Collection Resort, ushered in a new era of luxurious resort travel to Hawaii. The most coveted spot on Waikiki Beach is at The Royal Hawaiian — within the billowing sanctuary of private beachfront cabanas or from luxurious guest rooms showcasing unrivaled panoramic views of Diamond Head, Waikiki Beach, and the sparkling Pacific Ocean — we offer Hawaii's most majestic and memorable experiences."*

"No wonder you wanted to stay here; it sounds really nice. Oddly enough, I haven't been here before. I've only walked past. It's kind of tucked away from the main road. OK, I think we have arrived."

After the bellman collected the suitcases, Jenae pulled the car up to a temporary loading spot down the drive shaded by lush flowering bushes and palm trees. She escorted her parents into the main lobby to reception.

"Aloha, Welcome."

"Aloha, I'd like to check into my room, please."

"I see you have the Kamaaina rate. Do you have an ID?"

"Yes, here's my Hawaii driver's license. I work at the hospital as a nurse. I'm just taking a much needed respite during my parents' visit."

Jenae wasn't staying at the hotel but pulled off the story, so no questions were asked. The bellman led the trio to a luxury suite with the highest ceilings Jenae had ever seen in a hotel room. They were in the original building, which made the stay even more special.

"Can you join us for dinner tonight at the hotel? You can bring a friend." Mom said, hoping Jenae would return with an eligible young man.

"Sure, I'll return the car and then come back at about 6:30. Does that work for you?

"We will make a reservation at 6:45 for four people."

Jenae and Pami walked to the Royal Hawaiian in the best attire that they could muster up that didn't resemble beachwear or club fashion. Jenae borrowed a dowdy sundress from Pami for the occasion.

"It's very nice to meet you! I got to meet your son, Niles, last month and now Jenae's parents," Pami said.

"I'm surprised you never met in San Antonio. Pami and I have been friends for a long time," Jenae said.

"We're glad we are meeting you now. Look at the surfers out there with the sunset behind them. Sitting at a table right next to the ocean at a beautiful hotel; this really is paradise," Mom said.

"Let's order drinks. Do you know what you want to have for dinner?" Dad asked.

The table ordered enough food for Jenae to take home the leftovers.

"You girls have made the most of nursing — it looks like to me. I mean, I wish they had something like this when I was a young nurse. Aren't you glad you went into nursing, like your mama?" Mom said.

"I can thank Pami for hooking me up in Hawaii. It was her idea. The nursing profession has been a good fit for me. My RN is great; it's challenging, and I can find a job pretty much anywhere I want nowadays. The pay could always be better."

Mom was proud to call her daughter a nurse, but Jenae had really wanted to go to medical school and be a doctor like her father. Her parents, and most of society, had subtly and not so subtly discouraged her from being a *boss girl*. Men traditionally filled the majority of medical school admission seats. Jenae felt that her parents wanted her to *marry* a doctor, not *be* a doctor.

"Are you seeing anybody here? Niles told us that you have a love interest."

"Oh no. That's pretty much finished."

"Jenae! What happened this time? Niles said that he liked him and that he's a good-looking Marine with a nice family. Will you ever find anyone good enough?" Mom said.

Jenae turned red with embarrassment and anger and bit her lip as she looked down to readjust her napkin on her lap. Pami kept her head down and grabbed another roll to butter.

Mom continued, "Can't you find a nice doctor at the hospital?"

"You'd think, but the interns and residents that I know are un-dateable and they don't do anything fun because they are married to their education and on-call shifts at the hospital. It would be like marrying a ghost if I fell for a doctor. No offense, Dad."

"Your grandfather was a Marine in World War One. He found your Russian grandmother after the war. You know, I grew up in a middle-class apartment when they settled down. And even though he became a professor at the university for stability, we were poor, like many other families during that time. My advice is that when you are looking for the next guy, remember that you can marry more money in ten minutes than you can make in a lifetime." Her father's joking words were intended to put her mind at ease. But somehow, it made her feel like a commodity. After drinks and dinner, Dad signed the check. Jenae packed up the leftovers, and her parents took their jet-lagged bodies back to their luxury suite. Pami didn't have much to say to Jenae on the walk back to their condo except for, "Dang, you weren't kidding when you said your mom is hard on you."

The twenty-five-minute flight to the Big Island was more than transportation; it was a sightseeing expedition. Jenae and her mom sat on the side of the plane that gave the best views, according to the flight attendant. Their small plane quickly banked after takeoff, which gave a scary but perfect sight of the waves breaking along the shoreline. The islands in the distance seemed close, but not close enough to warrant a boat ferry system.

The Island of Hawaii was nicknamed The Big Island because it's the biggest island in the chain, and also the newest island with an active volcano still spewing lava. A fine line of smoke was visible from a crater as the commuter flight followed the beach before turning to the airport to land.

"Wow, that was a fast flight. I barely had time to finish my POG cup. What is POG anyway?" Mom said.

It's a mixture of pineapple, orange, and guava juices mixed together. Pretty good, huh?"

"I do like it, sweet and refreshing. Where should we go first?"

"The volcano woke up and has been steaming this summer. We should go visit that first before she blows for real."

"Sounds like an adventure, Jenae. I'll make sure to get a map at the rental counter."

Driving on the Big Island from the Kona airport was akin to landing on an extraterrestrial planet. The landscape was black and rocky with no vegetation, and the dark blue ocean beat violently against the sharp edges of overhanging cliffs. Black lava absorbed the sun's heat, which gave off thick evaporative mirages on the tarry road ahead. A few white river rocks used in the construction of the roads were repurposed as a decorative graffiti media. Against the black lava landscape, white rocks were positioned to say *J+R = LUV* and *TAHITI OR BUST* along the main highway.

"I think we should stop somewhere and leave a message with some white rocks ourselves, Jenae. You know, a non-permanent homage to our visit."

"Wow, I never knew you were such a rebel, Mom."

"There's a lot you don't know about me because I don't want you to know. It was a different time and a different place."

"Ah, I suppose some things are meant to be kept close to the vest, as they say."

"Pull over here. I see some white rocks in a pile."

Jenae and her mom stopped along a wide shoulder of the road and scampered to the other side of the freeway to retrieve the white rocks. They filled the front of their shirts with as many as they could carry, and Jenae put a few in her pockets, too. A fifty-foot hike up the embankment was more difficult than they expected. Lava was not only porous, but sharp and jagged, too. After a few stumbles, they reached the perfect spot for their message, *MOM-DOT '88.* Jenae and her mom stepped away from the message to see it in perspective.

"It's PERFECT."

"I love it. How long do you think it will stay like that?"

"Hopefully, it will be here for a few years, but at least long enough for us to see it again when we come back to the airport in a few days."

The pair drove until they came upon an old-timey Hawaiian Village. It reminded Mom of *Cowtown* in her mid-western hometown. She thought of the many times she toured guests down the boardwalk to the saloon for a sarsaparilla (root beer), and watched actors perform gunfights in the middle of the dusty town.

The Hawaiian museum was much more chill, with a ukulele player singing under a tree and a group of elders weaving baskets in a hut. Captain Cook was the only villain depicted on historical information posts looking out on the ocean. Disease brought to the islands by ships of explorers killed more Hawaiians than gunfights did in the Dustbowl era.

Music resonated from a small chapel up the hill. The small steeple building held no more than twenty people. Mom and Jenae peered into the open door from a respectable distance to get a glance of a couple standing on the altar, saying their "I dos." "I now pronounce you husband and wife." Claps and music erupted shortly before the bride and groom emerged onto the front porch, holding hands. He was a local dressed in a Hawaiian shirt and dark pants, while she was probably a Haole-larger and taller and wore a fluffy white dress in full regale. The mom-dot pair got swept up in the joy of the moment as if they were invited guests. They smiled and clapped as the newlywed couple waved and gave hugs to their guests.

"How much do you want to bet she is about five months pregnant?" Jenae quipped.

"A lot of marriages start that way. Your father says that if you want to have children, you should get pregnant first, before the wedding. That way, the issue of infertility is off the table. As long as you're sure, of course."

"I'll keep that in mind, mom."

The wedding party continued the celebration at a private luau set up next to the beach and Jenae and Mom hit the road.

Chapter 20

Biggest Rock

A cliff face at the southern most point of the United States called Ka Lae was windy and awe-inspiring. The ladies walked down a well-beaten path made by hikers and horses. A horseback riding tour had recently passed the same way and left behind fresh and fragrant manure plops along the way.

Once they reached the cliff face, they gazed out at the endless Pacific Ocean. All that was separating them from Antarctica was thousands of miles of deep blue water. A local rancher approached the pair and gave them a quick explanation of the area. He attested that Ka Lae was an excellent fishing spot; however, swimming there was not advised due to the steep, forty-foot rocky cliffs, deep waters, and dangerous undercurrents. The current, known as "Halaea," would sweep any daredevils straight out to sea. It was named after a Hawaiian chief whose fate was a watery grave at that very location. Just west of South Point, Papakolea, (also known as Green Sand Beach), had a better reputation for safe swimming. They spied a sole bald man snorkeling in the small bay below from their view on the cliffs above. The two-mile trek to Green Sand Beach, named for green volcanic olivine crystals that make up the sand, was only for hardcore adventurers, the rancher explained.

"This is Ka Lae. It's the first place Polynesians came ashore when they reached the Hawaiian Islands at about 750 A.D. Look down there; you can see old canoe mooring holes carved throughout the rocks. Fishermen still use them today."

In contrast, a windmill farm was poised on the southern point of Ka Lae. Massive white oscillating structures looked out of place, but futuristic, as one of the first of its kind in the country.

"What's the deal with the windmills up there? I've never seen anything like it," Jenae asked.

"We don't know what to make of those monstrosities. I know my cattle stay clear of them. This is one of the windiest places on earth and the government and the power company say it provides electricity for all the other islands."

"It sounds like an incredible source of energy. I wonder what the downside might be."

"Who knows? Where are you going next?"

"I think we're headed up to Volcanoes National Park to have a look around."

"Keep your head on a swivel. Kilauea has been burping and sneezing lately. She may be ready for a big release soon."

"Let's hope she waits a few days until we're gone."

The rancher shook his head and turned to walk away. He waved goodbye with his hat in hand. "Have a good visit."

"Thanks for talking to us."

The road to Volcanoes National Park wound through a lush rain forest where Jenae and Mom parked alongside the road to walk through lava tubes reminiscent of tunnels blasted into the side of mountains. Darkness in the black, shiny tube disoriented the pair, and Jenae's mild case of claustrophobia kicked in. They turned around to exit and kept their balance by holding onto the side of the tube. Mom heard Jenae yell out a shriek.

"Are you OK? What is going on?"

Jenae's heart pounded when she accidentally ran into a large man as she turned around.

"Oh, I'm so sorry. I didn't know you were behind me. I can't see a thing."

"No problem, I'll just scoot around you. I can barely see myself," said the stranger.

"Let's hurry up and get the heck out of here."

"For sure, we should have bought a flashlight for this."

The pair were on high alert after the warning the rancher had given them.

"Anything could have happened in there and nobody would have heard our screams or anything." Jenae sprinted to the car ahead of Mom.

The walk around the rim of Kilauea Volcano took mom and dot on a path of native plants and trees with rainbow bark. High humidity created a mist in the jungle, and hot sulfuric vapors around the volcano's edge made the area smell of rotten eggs. A yellow crust had formed on the ridge and Jenae couldn't get the urge to race away out of her gut.

"This is just amazing, isn't it, honey? Look down into the bottom of the crater. Steam is coming out of the center."

"Doesn't that make you nervous? It makes me nervous."

"It's been like this for a gazillion years. What are the odds that it would erupt while we're here?"

"Probably small, but..."

"Let's just walk a bit further around the rim. I want to take some pictures from a different perspective. This'll probably be the last time your old mama will be here to visit."

"OK, Mom. Let's take some pictures near the vent holes."

This may be the last time anybody visits this spot.

The hotel on an overlook of the black, rocky beach was an assurance to Jenae that she would survive the weekend excursion with her mother, who was willing to take more chances than her. At the hotel restaurant, they dined on a fish and chicken platter along with a few rounds of umbrella drinks.

"I see they have helicopter rides to the volcanoes. Should we take one tomorrow? I've only ridden in a helicopter one time."

"That's one more time than me, Mom, and I'll be happy to never ride in a helicopter in this lifetime."

"There's a Captain Cook snorkeling tour out of a bay near here. I can call for a reservation."

"I'd love to go, but I may just watch you snorkel. I don't feel comfortable swimming in the big ocean."

"A toast to us... Polar opposites."

———◦———

Seven AM came early for their snorkel trip to Kealakekua Bay on a Zodiac boat. Half a dozen other tourists boarded the boat with Jenae and Mom. The Aussie Captain's instruction to don and buckle life jackets was prudent especially for the speed and bounce-ability of the inflated side seating. Mom held onto the rope attached to the boat and whooped and hollered while her hair trailed horizontally and sea spray tingled her face. Her eyes widened each time her bountiful bottom bounced up and down. The Aussie Captain had a reputation to maintain of arriving first to Captain Cook's cove; his special mooring spot gave his clients the closest view of the monument and time to enjoy the reef without others around.

His promise of viewing dozens of different varieties of tropical fish was fulfilled, along with a couple of "Honu" lounging on the sandy bottom. The Captain explained that it was a turtle cleaning station where fish would pick off small barnacles while the turtles hung out. It resembled a carwash line under the sea.

On a small peninsula, easily viewed from the boat, sat Captain Cook's Monument that looked like a mini-Washington Monument in D.C.. The Aussie Captain was a master storyteller recounting the atrocities of the time.

"There are few places in all of Hawaii more historic than Kealakekua Bay, and this is the very spot where Captain Cook was killed in a skirmish with native Hawaiians. On February 14, 1779, Native Hawaiians killed the great English explorer and navigator during his third visit to the Pacific Island group.

A little background about Cook... In 1768, he started a commission in the Royal Navy to chart the course of the planet Venus. That expedition took scientists to Tahiti, and on a three-year journey; he explored the coast of New Zealand and Australia and circumnavigated the globe before returning to England.

After years of exploration extending to Antarctica, he made his first visit to the Hawaiian Islands in 1778. He may have been the first European ever to visit the island group, which he named the Sandwich Islands, in honor of one of his patrons, John Montague, the Earl of Sandwich. European ships fascinated the Hawaiians, as well as their use of iron. They welcomed Captain Cook and his crew. Cook provisioned his ships by trading metal, and his sailors traded iron nails for sex. After an expedition to the Northwest Passage, Cook's two ships returned to the Hawaiian Islands and found a safe harbor right here in Hawaii's Kealakekua Bay.

Hawaiians attached religious significance to Cook's visits here. Kealakekua Bay was considered the sacred harbor of Lono, the fertility god of the Hawaiians, and at Cook's first arrival, the locals were engaged in a festival dedicated to Lono. Captain Cook and his compatriots were welcomed as gods, and for the next month, they exploited the Hawaiians' goodwill.

However, Cook's arrival brought infectious diseases that devastated the Native Hawaiian population because they had no immunity to the communicative contagions. They'd never been exposed to white man's bacteria and viruses. Cook's omnificent bubble burst when one of their crewmen died, which exposed the Europeans as mere mortals. The ship left the angry islanders behind, but after a week of rough seas in the winter of 1779, the expedition was forced to return to Hawaii.

The Hawaiians greeted Cook and his men by hurling rocks, and they stole a small cutter vessel right off this shore. There were negotiations with King Kalaniopuu for the return of the cutter, but those collapsed after a lesser Hawaiian chief was shot to death. Hawaiians attacked Cook's party, and Captain Cook himself was killed. Native Hawaiians view the monument not to commemorate Cook's expedition and life but to mark the end of a mortal and cultural threat."

On the ride back from snorkeling, the boat hugged the volcanic coast at a reasonable pace and maneuvered into blue caves and lava tubes that were only accessible by their small Zodiac boat. The caves were hit with waves of water, which added excitement as the skilled boat captain maneuvered through confined spaces. As dolphins escorted the boat back to Kona, the Captain told a story of lifesaving dolphin pods that protected humans from shark attacks.

"OK folks, *Now that you are out of the water, I can tell you this story. When I was a young buck in Australia, my mate was riding behind our boat, holding onto the end of a rope for fun. Kind of like a water skier, but he was lying on the water's surface. It's really stupid to think about now because he resembled a big piece of bait on a line. I looked back from driving the boat and saw him thrown in the air with his arms straight up, and then he fell into his own pool of bloody water. He didn't move, and I thought he was dead, but our other mate took a dingy out to rescue him. As he approached, he saw two fins circling our friend's lifeless body. They were dolphin fins, and the shark that had just attacked him was nowhere to be seen. The shark attack stopped when those dolphins showed up. So always feel privileged when dolphins are in sight. They are compassionate animals.*"

"Oh, my goodness. Did your friend survive?" Jenae asked.

"He did. The scars are crazy, but he's grateful to be alive."

Right on cue, two dolphins who had been swimming on each side of the boat jumped out of the water to spy on the human visitors and to bid them, Aloha.

The mom-dot pair split up in the afternoon after the Aussie Captain offered to sign anyone up who wanted to scuba dive the lava tubes. Jenae couldn't pass up a once-in-a-lifetime opportunity to watch lava seep into the ocean to form a new land mass. Mom had different ideas and had a van pick her up at the hotel for an afternoon helicopter ride to view all five volcanic craters, waterfalls, and ocean-side cliffs.

An old, retired military pilot flew the helicopter – which included headphones – so Mom and the other three passengers could communicate and hear the narratives of Mauna Loa's Puna rainforests, mesmerizing Hilo waterfalls, and black sand beaches. Mom felt a strong camaraderie with the other passengers and enjoyed the communal energy of imagining what could happen in a small metal bird dipping into valleys and volcanoes and nearly swiping the cliff's sides. She squealed and hooted as others clutched onto the handles when the helicopter banked for optimal views.

While Mom was in the air, Jenae was on a fancy dive boat preparing to go below the ocean's surface. The teakwood and brass finishes created an upscale vibe, which was usually not a part of most dive boats. It had an inner cabin with sleeping bunks and a small galley. The owner, captain, and dive master of the boat brought his prized possession out of dock specifically to dive the active lava that flowed into the ocean. A young man wearing a *Just Mauied* T-shirt and his mom had recently gotten their scuba certifications back home on the mainland and it was their first vacation dive.

Each diver backed off the rear of the boat on wooden steps between two large engines and sunk into the calm waters near shore. A boat photographer was Jenae's dive buddy. The picture lady swam to each dive couple and took pictures of them in their masks and regulators, flashing the obligatory *hang loose* sign.

Black lava steamed under the ocean as Jenae and the picture lady closed in at a 50-foot depth. The thrill of seeing something completely new and dangerous gave Jenae an unexpected sense of peacefulness. She took in slow easy breaths provided by the oxygen tank strapped to her back, and her gaze wandered and focused on the lava's slow expansion onto the bottom of the ocean. The synchronicity of nature played out beautifully while schools of fish gravitated to the steamy, warm water as if it were a communal hot tub.

Jenae felt more in touch with her true self as she recalled a recent tarot card reading, "Pisces often feel more harmonious in the water, soothing their emotions by creating a bubble of protection from the rest of the world."

Chapter 21

I Spy

The view from a high-rise condo with reflective glass was unobstructed from the 17th floor into an apartment at the Kaipuna across the street. Two large lens cameras were pointed at the front bedroom and main living area. Three women and one man were posing for pictures on a Kaipuna balcony. "She looks like she's with a different guy." Agents kept watch over their target.

Logan arrived solo by cab to the apartment high in the sky for a special assignment. He'd mostly slept on the five-hour flight after an overnight surveillance assignment in Brentwood. He and another agent from the Los Angeles bureau were summoned to Honolulu because of their youthful good looks and their reputation for seductive aptitudes.

"Welcome to the most entertaining gig we have had in a while, gentlemen. Our target is this apartment primarily, but we're watching the entrances, garages and pedestrian traffic as well. The three ladies that occupy this residence don't pull their curtains – ever. So we have 24-7 visuals," the lead investigator said.

"We need to figure out this situation. This team has been here for a month and so far all we have are a bunch of fake bomb threats in the middle of the night called in from a local army base," he continued.

"I don't mind coming to Hawaii for a few weeks. LA was getting boring, and it's nice to have a change of scenery. Who are the main suspects, boss?" Logan asked.

"We know that a woman in this apartment has had communication with the suspect from the base. She's in her twenties, 5-foot 8-inches – 5-foot 10-inches tall, slender, and has brown hair. She works at a local hospital as a travel nurse but hasn't been seen there in the past week. This gal on the balcony fits the description, and this is the first we've seen of her in a while.

All the women are residents in this apartment and are contracted with the same travel nurse agency. We aren't sure if it is her boyfriend or her brother who works on base. Maybe both. They haven't given us much information lately from the trackers and phone taps.

We have an overlap of teams for the next few days, and I'm setting up an operation to follow two of the suspects. According to their conversation, they're going out to the local bars tonight. This might open up the case for us if we can get them drinking and talking."

"How many guys are going out tonight to try to honey-pot these girls?"

"At least four of us. Two of us old married guys can monitor the phones and cameras."

"Ah, good. It'll be a competition for the manliest pickup lines. By the way, why didn't the local office handle this investigation?" Logan asked.

"A couple of reasons. First, they didn't want to be identified by locals because they don't know whom they are dealing with. More importantly, the national implications of the suspect coming from a US military base made this investigation a need-to-know basis only. It could be part of a bigger terrorist threat that we've been working on. We have direct communication with the management of the Kaipuna and just a few higher-ups at the Bureau here."

"My mom is taking a cab to the airport this afternoon to go back home. She is stopping by here first to say goodbye," Jenae told Pami.

"Oh good, I didn't get to see her much after our dinner with her and your dad at the Royal Hawaiian. I've been working too hard, and you've been playing too hard with your guests."

"Mom wanted to see Walker before she left, too, so he'll be stopping by in a few minutes."

"Great, I'll get a few pictures for you if you want. Our balcony view would be better without that big shiny building next door, but we can get a side view of the ocean if we angle it just right. How are you feeling after the whole Tim and Hannah affair?"

"Well, I still hate them both, of course. If I had a car and saw them walking in front of me, I would step on the gas and then throw it into reverse and step on the gas again. Babump, babump...babump, babump."

Pami laughed, "It's a good thing you only have that stupid scratched up bike. The damage record is 0-1 with that thing. I do like the visual of you throwing the car in reverse though, that's good revenge action. Would you look over your shoulder or just in the rearview mirror when you backed over your victims the second time?"

"Not sure, that's something I'll have to think about."

"I'm glad you moved in with me, Jenae. I haven't seen Hannah at all, even at work. I am sure she is embarrassed about sleeping with Tim. I'm still not sure what happened with Ronin."

"I just don't care anymore. My heart's been broken, but the rule is it only takes two weeks to mend it again, right?"

"That's right, except in Dean's case, it only took you two hours."

"Good point, but I'd been planning that break up for a long time."

"Hey, so after your mom goes to the airport, let's get really dolled up in our hottest outfits, go out to the bars and pick up some men. It's just you and me tonight, and we're going to find the smartest, richest, sexiest, most built guys visiting the island this week."

"You are on!"

———————◄O►———————

Jenae emerged from her bedroom after primping her hair with mousse and applying her makeup. She even ironed her white cotton midriff top with a can of starch she found in the cabinet, left over from the mystery roommate. She wore tight fitting black pants and black sandals with her newly painted red toenails, which lead slow, confident steps into the living room.

"Va va va voom," Pami said and smiled. "Look at you!"

"Thanks, I usually don't wear long pants here, but since we are taking it up a notch, I thought why not?"

"I think you would look good in anything with your new athletic, tanned body. I've never seen you this fit before."

"I can thank the triathlon training for that. And I'm so glad it's over. It almost killed me. Ugh. Now I can focus on fun without the guilt and stress of workouts."

"Yeah, I cannot relate Jenae. The only running I do is for the bus when I'm late."

"Pami, you always rock those linen shorts cinched up at your tiny waist. I'm jealous. Oh, and I love the halter top, too."

"Thanks. I had to get a special bra for this thing."

Confidence was on the rise with the best friends and looking the part of naughty nurses didn't hurt their cause.

Chapter 22

New Attitude

Pami led the way as she and Jenae popped out of the stairs onto the balcony bar. "Moose's seems extra crowded tonight."

"Let's walk around and see if we can find a table by the dance floor," Jenae said.

After a stop at the bar, both ladies double-fisted two large hurricane glasses filled with vodka, tequila, light rum, triple sec, gin, and a splash of cola (AKA a Long Island Iced Tea). Jenae and Pami made a visual inspection of the entire bar with a deliberate promenade between tables while sipping on straws and moving with the beat of the live band. There were no seats available, but there were an unusually large number of young men with very short haircuts and cheesy grins smiling at them as they sauntered past.

"I guess we're going to have to take over one of these military guys' tables," Jenae said.

"We should feel bad about doing this, but it works every time. Go get that one; those guys look naïve enough." Pami pointed to a high-top table with four airmen perched up like meerkats; with their necks cranked toward them to get a better look. They appeared to be the ripe old age of 23 and had just graduated from the Air Force Academy, but clearly hadn't been participants in football, basketball, rugby, or the swim team.

"So, what are you guys doing in Hawaii? Are you on vacation?" Jenae asked.

"A little bit of fun, but mostly work. We are on a TDY – that is a temporary duty station away from our base."

"What do you do?"

"We're pilots in the Air Force, well, except for that guy with the glasses; he's a navigator."

"That sounds really cool. Are you having a good time so far?"

"Certainly are. Would you like to sit at our table?"

"That is so polite of you, thank you. Are you sure?"

"Absolutely. It looks like you need a spot to set those big drinks down."

Pami and Jenae plopped down on the bar chairs and laughed and cajoled with the airmen, using their best flirtation techniques just long enough to justify their commandeered table.

"Ladies, I apologize for the interruption, but I need to take these gentlemen back to their hotel. We have an early show time tomorrow." An older airman appeared out of nowhere and escorted the First Lieutenants to a white van waiting on the street below.

"Bye! It was nice to meet you. Good luck with everything." The girls waved.

"Well, that was easy. Now let's find some real men."

Across the room, a table of plainclothes FBI agents watched the young women and made a plan.

"These ladies are taller than I expected; all of us are under 6-foot, so who has the best game?"

"Logan, you take the lead. At least you are 5'7". The rest of us will hang back and wait for your signal to join the table."

"I'm 5'9" – by the way – and this is going to be like taking candy from a baby. Are you sure I get paid for this?"

"Show us what you've got, big guy."

"Here goes nothing."

The girls were bopping along with the music from the cover band, and Pami had just sucked the last few drops away from the ice at the bottom of her second Long Island Iced Tea glass. They were feeling tipsy and flirty when an average looking clean-cut guy in his early 30s approached their table. He leaned in with a gleam in his eye and offered witty commentary on the ratio of men to women in the bar.

"I know I can't compete with all the good-looking young military guys in here, but can I buy you ladies a drink?"

"Oh, hi, sure. What is your story? Who are you with?"

"I'm here with my buddies over there." Logan pointed to the other agents watching him, and they waved back.

"Ah, did they leave their wives back at the hotel?" Pami asked suspiciously.

Logan barely met the physical height and good looks standards of Pami and Jenae, and the rest of the table definitely did not come close. Conversation was sparse and boring with the "accountant from Torrance." The undercover FBI agent was intimidated by the ladies aloofness and especially by Pami's side eye. Halfway through the drink, the ladies were ready to move on.

"Well, thanks for the drinks. It was nice to meet you."

"Yeah, nice to meet you, too. Maybe we can dance a little later," Logan said.

Jenae smiled and nodded.

"OK, who's next? I have had my eye on a really good-looking tall guy in the corner back there. I think he winked at me earlier," Pami said.

"Go over and talk to him. I'll stay here and save the table."

The FBI agents at the table nearby dressed down Agent Logan as they sipped on their club sodas with lime.

"Are you losing your touch, Logan?"

"You just got shut down. It was ugly!"

"Only after they got a glimpse of you losers. I mean, look at this place – it's crawling with studs. I think it's pretty easy for them to overlook the Old Spice crowd."

"If only they knew we listened to their conversations, watched them sleep, undress, and have sex."

"Dude, you are supposed to turn off the visuals during intimate moments." Logan looked dismayed.

"We have enough footage to make a VHS porn movie – by accident, of course. I'm going to the bathroom to see what that girl is doing in the corner with that big guy. It sounds like he has an accent from here. Not sure if he's British or Australian."

From a distance, they observed every movement the ladies made, as well as each person who talked or danced with them. The best-case scenario would be that the boyfriend or brother show up and they could start a tail on them since they were clueless on whom the suspects really were. The second option had been blown for that night; the girls were already talking to multiple guys and Logan was not getting a dance. The FBI wanted to interrogate the girls on the down low, incognito, under the pretense of a date or a hook-up. They may have struck out on this night, but the challenge had not vanquished completely.

Having personal conversations with strangers was second nature for most nurses, and these girls easily converted it into seductive banter at the bar. Pami identified her prince charming and turned on her own charm.

"So, what do you do for fun in New Zealand? It sounds so exotic." Pami loved the sound of Karl's accent; she could listen to his slightly slurred speech all night. And he was tall, good looking, and fit.

"For fun, I go out to the west coast of the South Island and hike with my mates on most weekends. We stay at a cabin out there. I love to eat seafood, too. Have you ever had New Zealand mussels? They are the big green-lipped ones."

"I've only eaten oysters. Are they like that?"

"Yeah, yeah, the shells are thicker and the meat is fleshier. We have brilliant fish and seafood, obviously, because we're an island nation."

"Mm sounds delicious. You said you were a police officer? What's it like being a cop? Was it dangerous?"

"My mate, Neve, the one who is piss drunk talking to that girl over there, he and I were in the police force together in Christchurch on the South Island. He's good as gold."

"So, I presume there is a North Island, too?"

"Yeah, yeah. Two big islands make up the bulk of New Zealand."

"I got off track. So tell me about how brave you were."

"It was exciting being a police officer, especially fresh out of the academy; learning to shoot and implementing tactical and investigative techniques. Neve and I were on some exciting assignments together, but the adrenaline rush isn't sustainable, and I want something more stable. That's what this trip is about. I'm changing course and getting into property development. My cousin is in the business and Neve flips real estate, too."

"How long are you here?"

"This is the last two-week leg of our two-month vacation to the States. We've been in Hawaii for just two days. Yeah, that means we have almost two weeks left; my brain is swimming in alcohol, too much to do the math."

Pami turned away and burst into laughter, but quickly leaned into Karl and smiled. She was planning the next date with Karl in her mind as she locked eyes with his, took his hand, and asked him to dance as the band started a slow, romantic song.

Jenae saw Pami swaying back and forth hanging on a tall guy in front of the band stage, but was distracted by a group of friends from Boston who had just graduated from business school. She let them move in on her table because she had a lot of questions for these men about their MBA experience. They were kind of cute, too.

"How did you get into such a prestigious school? You really went to an Ivy League college?" Jenae asked as she leaned on her planted elbows on the table and made full contact with Johnny's dark brown eyes.

"Well, yeah, I went to undergrad at a private college on the East Coast and was lucky to get admitted, honestly. My dad had to pull a few strings."

"What's the thing that you are most proud of while you were in business school?"

"At this moment, probably just graduating and getting a well paid job. I am going to work as an international broker for racehorses. But the best part of grad school was making new friends and networking. This trip to Hawaii is just some guys and girls from our class that wanted to celebrate."

"I've never even thought about race horses needing to be traded. I suppose horse trading is one of the oldest professions, huh?"

"Horse racing is big on the East Coast. We have a lot of prestigious stables. What do you want to do with an MBA? You already have a good job in nursing, right?"

"Probably work in administration or get away from the hospital and try out the business side of healthcare. I love taking care of patients, but I need to push and challenge myself to really be happy."

It became clear that Boston Johnny didn't have the same upbringing and education as Jenae:

Private schools vs. Public schools;

East coast vs. Midwestern;

Vacation to Hawaii vs. Working in Hawaii;

Family funded education vs. College loans;

Well connected vs. Starting from scratch.

However, Hawaii seemed to be a leveling agent that brought up-and-coming people together from all over the world. Jenae was hopeful that her summer of '88 would be enriched by the wide array of young, bright successful folks who celebrated on the big rock in the Pacific.

Chapter 23

Love Blooms

Although Johnny had lived his entire existence on the East Coast, he had a strong attraction to middle-of-the-country Jenae. She was from the heartland and beamed with a warm heart and beauty that Johnny longed for in a future wife. He bought her drinks and danced with her the rest of the night.

Pami disappeared shortly after she was seen in a full-out make-out session on the dance floor with Kiwi Karl.

Johnny and his friend Boston Bob walked her home down busy Kalakaua Avenue in the warm, midnight, tropical air. Illuminations and hullabaloo from the big city bustle, perfume from tropical flowers, and the soft, sultry breeze gave tourists the energy to stay out late to soak up as much paradise as possible. It was the natural version of oxygen being pumped into casinos that kept gamblers at the tables into the wee hours of the morning.

A popular nightclub across the street from the Kaipuna was hopping as usual. Most nights, the music and rotating spotlights emanated from a heavy steel side door as patrons were allowed in one by one after passing the "cool enough to enter" test by two large bouncers.

"Hey, let's go to this night club. I think I heard about it from our group. They may be inside and it's open late," Boston Bob said.

"It's very popular, and there's always a line to get inside. You and Johnny should go. I probably need to head in and get some sleep," Jenae said.

"Yeah, OK sure. You get in line, Bob, and I'll walk Jenae back to her apartment. I'll join you before you get in the front door."

Johnny and Jenae walked across the street and hugged goodnight at the front entrance of the Kaipuna after Jenae gave him her number. He was an upstanding guy, and she decided to change tact in her dating strategy and give him a chance, even though he didn't ignite her carnal passions.

Across the street, tall, dark, and handsome Boston Bob stood in line with a group of hot girls in mutual admiration. Earlier at Moose's, Bob made it very clear that he had a serious girlfriend at home; however, that didn't stop him from flirting with every girl that passed by.

———◆———

Pami wandered into the Kaipuna apartment at the break of dawn. She and Kiwi Karl had drifted into a few other bars in Waikiki and ended up falling asleep on the beach after the alcoholic beverages killed their libidos. Karl's friend Neville (Neve for short) put Pami in a cab after they made it back to the Kiwis' hotel room.

At noon, Jenae checked Pami's room to make sure she had made it back OK. The phone rang.

"Hello?" Jenae answered the phone call.

"Aloha! It's Johnny from last night. Is this Jenae?"

"Yes, don't you recognize my voice? Did you forget it already?"

"Not likely. How'd you sleep?"

"I tossed and turned a little, but pretty good overall. How about you, Johnny? Did you get your full eight hours?"

"It was a short night. We were at the club until they kicked us out at 3 AM. Our friends from business school were there, just as Bob thought, and it got pretty crazy. Our room looks like a bomb went off, and I think Bob ended up making out with a guy dressed up as a lady in a parked car last night."

"What? Did he know it was a guy?"

"I'm pretty sure he didn't. In Bob's defense, he looked really hot in a mini-skirt and high heels."

"Then how did Bob know he wasn't a woman?"

"I think there was some crotch action that revealed more than a woman would have down there."

"So he touched a man's penis. That is hilarious. His serious girlfriend at home is going to love that story."

"I don't think Bob plans on his girlfriend finding out anything that has happened here after dark."

"Warn him that women have a way of finding these things out."

"I'll prepare him for an emanate break up when he gets back to Boston. Hey, I was wondering if you want to go out with me tonight. We have a rental car for a few more days, and I was hoping you could show me some other parts of the island."

"Alright, that should be fun. I can't stay out too late because I have an early shift in the morning."

"OK, great. Maybe we can catch the sunset, someone told me about a cool beach we can go to. I'll pick you up at seven-ish?"

"Alright, see you then."

Pami heard the phone conversation from her bedroom and yelled for Jenae to come lay down in bed with her to debrief the long night. Jenae grabbed two cans of POG and a box of wheat thins and gently lay down on the end of the bed, perpendicular to Pami's curled-up body.

"Here, drink this. The sugar might help your brain. It looks like you had a rough night."

"Can you shut the curtains for me? The light is too bright. Why don't we ever close these curtains?"

"Too lazy, I guess. So what's the story with this redwood tree-sized man that I saw you making out with on the dance floor last night?"

"I don't remember much except for waking up shivering on the beach with Karl passed out next to me."

"You left the table to talk to him, and before I had time to meet him, you were both stumbling down the stairs, and you never came back."

"Those drinks were really strong last night. I felt like I was drugged."

"Well, thank goodness you made it home in one piece. Could Karl have put something in your drink?"

"I don't think he'd do that. Besides, he acted like he was drugged, too. Maybe someone at the bar did it."

"Oh yeah, like the creepy friends of Logan. They gave me the heebie jeebies."

"One of those guys came lurking around the bathroom close to where Karl and I were talking."

"That's scary."

"I think I like Karl, and he did ask me to hang out with him again. His friend Neve wanted me to bring you along for a double date."

"Who's Neve?"

"He's Karl's friend from New Zealand. His real name is Neville, but with their accent and nicknames, he goes by Neve. You know, Neve like Steve. I didn't realize it, but he saw you at Moose's last night, and this morning he suggested we go on a double date."

"I never saw this guy. What does he look like, and how tall is he?"

"He's definitely shorter than Karl, but he's over six feet tall. And he's a really good-looking guy with blue eyes and brown hair. He's cuter than Karl. I think you'd like him, and Karl says he is a good guy."

"I don't know. I met Boston Johnny last night, and he asked me to go out tonight."

"Well, you can walk and chew gum at the same time, can't you? Go out with both. The Kiwis are going to be here for at least another week and a half. We can schedule them on our next day off. Please, please, please? I promise Neve is really cute."

Johnny called Jenae from the front door at the Kaipuna, and she met him at his rental car parked on the street out front. She glanced over to the garden area where she and Tim first kissed and felt a pang in her heart. Johnny looked shorter and more East Coast than last night; maybe because she had taken off her beer goggles. They drove through Waikiki toward Diamond Head with the windows open as Jenae gave him directions to a beach that he had picked out on a map.

"One of the girls in our group told me about this place; she thought you might enjoy a new spot," Johnny said.

"I must really trust you taking me to a secluded beach on a first date after just meeting you last night."

"Ah, come on Jenae, I'm a good guy and very well behaved. I picked up some wine and cheese and crackers so that we can have a picnic and watch the sunset on a cool little beach."

"Just in case I go missing, my girlfriends know who I am going out with and they're skilled with sharp objects."

"Got it. I'm a really nice guy. You'll see."

Jenae had never walked down the cliff side to this beach off of Diamond Head, but she recognized it as a popular windsurfing spot during the day. She'd passed by it many times on her bike training rides. Johnny held her hand as Jenae gingerly navigated the steep rock and brush trail down to the coastline forty feet below. The sand area of the beach was small because the tide had come in, and there were two other couples sitting on blankets cuddled together.

Johnny laid down a blanket that he borrowed from his hotel room equidistant from the other couples and methodically opened the cheese and cracker packages as if he were setting up a photo shoot. With the sun setting, he twisted off the top of a bottle of red wine and poured it into two clear plastic cups.

"Cheers!"

"Cheers. Thanks for taking me out. I thought I'd be showing you new areas of the island, not the other way around. This is really nice."

Jenae felt safer with the other couples nearby and enjoyed learning more about Johnny and his family. He had a stable, marrying type of feel to him that was appealing to Jenae, and she was willing to explore it more, even though she didn't feel an animal attraction toward Johnny.

Johnny maneuvered behind Jenae so she could lean against his lower legs as they gazed at the horizon while the orange sun sunk into the ocean. As it got darker, Johnny wrapped his arms around her shoulders and gave her quick pecks on the cheek and neck from behind. Jenae never turned around for a full kiss and redirected his roaming hands off of her body.

"Oh, look – that couple is leaving. We should go too before it gets too dark." Jenae popped up off of the blanket and started packing up the picnic.

"You want to go so soon?"

"Yeah, I have work early in the morning and I should get back before it gets too late."

At the Kaipuna, Pami was knitting and talking on the phone with her dad about living expenses with the curtains wide open.

"Yes dad, I'm saving all of my receipts for the tax guy. I think I'll stay for another three-month contract when this one runs out. So, I'll be home at Christmas time for sure. I should have a nice nest egg built up by then. Love you, too. Take care. Bye Dad!"

"Where have you been?" Pami asked when Jenae walked in the door.

"I went on a date with that guy from Boston."

"You're home early. It must not have gone well, I suspect."

"Eh, it was alright. I mean, he's a nice guy, but probably not for me in the end. How are your mom and dad doing?"

"Pretty good. They plan on visiting me in the fall. Did I tell you that I'm staying here for another three months? I talked to my unit in San Antonio and they were fine with me coming back at the beginning of next year. I have no urgency to go back right now. I like the relaxed atmosphere here."

"Who else is staying? Hannah?" Jenae asked.

"Oh my God, I just heard the terrible news about Ronin. You know her boyfriend that dumped her or cheated on her or whatever. I'm not sure what the full story is," Pami replied.

"What happened to Ronin?"

"He's in the hospital. He had a horrible car accident about three weeks ago, and he's been in a coma ever since. Hannah called me tonight hysterical; she just found out about it. His roommate reached out to her because he hadn't seen Hannah at the hospital."

"What? How devastating. I saw Ronin about three weeks ago, right before I moved in with you."

"Where'd you see him?"

"He showed up at the door of my old apartment wanting to talk to Hannah. She wasn't there because she was probably down in Tim's apartment doing private lap dances. Anyway, I digress."

"What did Ronin want?"

"Maybe he wanted to repair their relationship. He left a note for her on her bed. He looked really distraught and said he hadn't slept all week. I think Ronin was upset about their breakup. I remember he asked me for some acetaminophen for a migraine. He decided not to go to work that night and was going to drive home."

"I wonder if that's the night he crashed!"

"Oh crap, I hope I didn't give him a sleeping pill instead of Tylenol."

Chapter 24

Intensive Care

A sterile ICU room on a separate wing from Jenae's work unit at the hospital had been home for Ronin since his devastating car crash that fateful night he had stopped by to find Hannah. Jenae may have been the last person to talk to him in a conscious state since then. She felt guilty that she'd been working in the same building the whole time without knowing that he was a patient. Hannah would have wanted to be there for him from the beginning, no matter the circumstance. Tragedy had a way of putting everything into perspective, including their damaged friendship.

Ronin's parents had immediately flown in from San Francisco and took every opportunity to sit at his bedside. They held his hand, avoiding the IV-tubing, and stroked his cheek around the breathing tube taped to his face. In a joyful voice, they reminisced about his childhood antics and told him stories about his friends and family back home. The time was limited, and never enough for his family to fully accept Ronin's dire situation. They prayed aloud to God to grant them the miracle of a full recovery, and that he would come back to them. Just last month, he was slaying the world with his business savvy and athleticism. He was in love with a girl for the first time since college. He was on top of the world – until he wasn't.

Pami escorted Hannah to the ICU the next morning for visiting hours. The shock and stress of seeing a loved one in such a state was debilitating. Hannah thought she passed Ronin's parents as they walked with slow, heavy steps down the shiny hallway. She couldn't be sure because she'd never met them in person, but she'd seen pictures at Ronin's house. Her vision was foggy, her eyes were red, and her face was puffy from crying all night and morning. Her heart was broken because she knew the final outcome would be bad no matter the medical intervention. Ronin's roommate told her on the phone that if Ronin ever woke up, he would be paralyzed from the waist down. He had broken vertebrae and a spinal cord injury. Pami sat Hannah down on a pleather-upholstered chair in an empty waiting room next to the elevators. She handed Hannah a box of tissues that were set on a table nearby.

"Here, sit for a moment while I ask this nurse about visitation."

"Ronin's parents just went in for a visit. They usually stay the whole two hours allowed," the ICU nurse said.

"Is there any way his girlfriend can see him today? Even for a few minutes? She just found out he was here last night, and she's devastated. We're both nurses at the children's hospital – if that helps."

"As you know, the rules are that only two visitors are allowed in the room at one time. Maybe I can stretch visiting hours another five minutes for her to go in after they leave. Are the parents expecting her?"

"No, they don't know she's here yet. Thank you so much. We'll wait here until his parents leave. Can you fill me in on his condition? We know he was involved in a single car accident in the mountains. Did he doze off and drift off the cliff?"

"I'm not sure what caused the accident. Let me grab his chart to see if he had any drugs or alcohol in his system."

"Thanks, that would be very helpful."

"Nope, his labs from his admission don't show any ETOH, opioids, or barbiturates."

"Well, that is reassuring. My other girlfriend saw him earlier that night of his accident and said he had a migraine and was having trouble sleeping."

"It sounds like he may have just fallen asleep at the wheel. He's been here for almost a month under sedation and we're hopeful that he'll wake up soon. The swelling in his brain and spine has subsided and we are just waiting for that spark to wake him up."

Hannah managed to avoid Ronin's parents when she was summoned by the nurse to come into his private, glassed-in room. Machines lit up surrounding his bed while a ventilator attached to a tube in his throat made his chest rise and fall in perfect measure.

"I can only give you a few minutes. He is doing better, and we've discontinued a lot of his medications. We are just waiting for him to wake up so we can take him off the ventilator."

"Thanks for letting me in. I can't believe this happened."

"I know, I'm so sorry. Take a few minutes now and you can come back when we can arrange it with the family to have more time."

"Ronin, are you in there? Can you hear me? It's Hannah; I got your note from that night, before you ran off the road. I'm sorry I was still so mad at you; I didn't know you were in the accident until last night. I love you Ronin, and I'll do everything for you if you come back to us. I will stay by your side while you recover. I'll make sure that you are OK. I know that your family loves you and wants you back. They've been here the whole time. Please come back to us, please."

Hannah held his hand and leaned in to kiss his forehead. A single tear rolled down his cheek.

Down the hall, Pami leaned against the telephone booth with the hospital house phone receiver to her ear and her hand cupped over her mouth.

"Hey, it's Pami."

"How's Ronin? Is Hannah OK?" Jenae answered on a work phone.

"I don't know. She is still in with him. His nurse is giving her only a few minutes to visit this morning, so she should be out soon."

"I'm freaking out! What if I gave him a sleeping pill instead of Tylenol for his migraine and that's why he crashed?" Jenae whisper-shouted into the receiver, careful that workmates weren't within listening distance.

"That's why I'm calling you. He didn't have any drugs or alcohol in his system when they brought him in. You did not cause his accident."

"Oh, thank the Lord! Are you sure? How do you know?"

"The nurse pulled his chart and showed me his toxicology results from that night. He must've just fallen asleep and veered off the road."

"I should have had him sleep here on the couch that night. Had I known..."

"Would of, could of, should of, Jenae...hindsight is 20/20. Don't blame yourself. You had nothing to do with this terrible tragedy."

"Thanks for calling me to put my mind at ease, but my head is still spinning. Maybe I will be able to concentrate on my patients a little bit better now."

"I'll take Hannah home and stay with her for a while to make sure she's alright. Maybe you two could talk again soon. She needs as much support as she can get right now."

"Sure thing, I'll walk over to ICU and check on Ronin on my lunch break today."

"Don't forget we have a day date planned with my New Zealand friends tomorrow. Hannah is coming down the hall now, gotta go. Bye."

"OK, you can fill me in on the details later. Bye, Bye."

Chapter 25

Surveillance or Stalking

Logan and the FBI team monitored phone calls to and from the apartment line, but the phone was rarely used. The most illegal dialogue they had listened in on was Pami's conversation with her father about her travel tax receipts. They did, however, carefully monitor Jenae's movements, including a slow drive behind her on her bike commute to and from work. They had watched her and Johnny from the overlook on their beach date. One of the agents stood in line next to her at the Jack in the Box while she waited for her order.

"Is the guy that we saw on the beach a suspect, or somebody different?" Logan asked his colleague.

"I wasn't here when those calls were made, but he fits the description in the report... six-foot tall, brown hair, brown eyes, medium build. The first bomb threat came from the phone number in this apartment. All the others were made from a pay phone on base."

"If they go out again, I want another bite at the apple to get an exchange with this girl. Let me know if you hear when and where they're going."

"Sure thing, boss," Logan said.

—◦—

Pami waited for Karl in the circle drive at the Kaipuna. She hadn't had a chance to tell Jenae that she was going out with Kiwi Karl for an early dinner. A taxi pulled up promptly at 5 PM. Karl unfolded his six-foot-five frame and jumped out. He was luscious to look at with broad shoulders, slim hips, meaty thighs, and light brown eyes.

"Let's go." He held the car door open for Pami as she scrambled into the back of the cab.

"Where are we going?"

"On a picnic, I got us poke bowls."

"Poke bowls?" Pami was not a fan of uncooked fish, but she was willing to try most anything once. She was wearing sensible shoes, as Karl had requested, but was suspicious that this would be a cheapskate dud date because it started out so weird. Who starts a date at 5 PM?

The cab crept along crowded Kalakaua Avenue, past Waikiki, into a residential district. "Here we are." "Here" was a tiny pocket beach park with only one teenager trying to ride some waves. It was quiet and beautifully landscaped.

Karl spread a clean beach towel over the top of a picnic table. He placed the poke bowls on top and magically produced a couple of beers from his bag.

"Let's go check out the beach before we eat." He grabbed Pami's hand and led her to some rocks nearby. Sitting close together on the rocks felt right. It had been a beautiful day with low humidity and a soft ocean breeze. The teen loaded up his board and disappeared on the path behind them. Karl turned toward Pami and cradled her face in his strong hands. "Hold on a second." He gently brushed her right cheek. "Sand." Pami closed her eyes in anticipation of a gentle kiss, but was slightly disappointed when Karl refrained.

After dinner, Pami looked around for potential new activities. "What's next?" She had confirmed her dislike for raw fish with her first bite, but enjoyed feeding Karl both bowls of poke with chopsticks. The chemistry was there, but Karl missed the mark on their compatibility.

"Since you didn't eat much dinner, let's get dessert."

Unlike Waikiki, things were much quieter at this end of the beach. She was surprised that they were within walking distance of anyplace selling dessert.

"I'm glad to see you're wearing your trainers, I mean sneakers, in Yank language."

"Yes, my super sexy sneakers," Pami said.

Karl slipped his arm around her slender waist and they sauntered down the path, making comfortable small talk, as if they had known each other in another lifetime. Soon enough they were at Kinani's, a tiny store that sold one of everything. They browsed in amazement at the variety of sundries.

"Look, here is a real coconut postcard. You can write a message on it and send it in the mail."

As Pami turned the corner, she pointed to a small freezer case that held ice cream bars.

"Is this where we're getting dessert?"

"No, maybe on our next date. I just wanted to stop in to get a box of Tic Tacs." He winked at Pami with an adorable smile.

They strolled past a beach known as Sans Souci.

"What does the name of that beach mean?" asked Karl.

"If my high school French class served me right, I'm going to guess that it means, No worries."

"Ah, a French Aussie must have named that beach. Hey, do you know the difference between Kiwis and Aussies? The Aussies are all criminals, and Kiwis are free people. We like to kid each other because we are cousin countries of the South Pacific; no, but really – Australia was a penal colony."

In the distance, a bride was having wedding photos taken amongst a soft sunset background. Pami imagined how she would look in a wedding gown herself, and more importantly, who would be her groom?

Karl and Pami people-watched and made up stories about them after they passed along the path.

"See that guy eating shaved ice on the bench? He's waiting for his wife to come out of that souvenir shop with a pair of prison shower shoes for him to wear at the gym back home in Cleveland, Ohio."

"What are prison shower shoes? Do you mean like the slides that athletes wear with white tube socks?"

"Exactly, except these are cooler because they look Hawaiian. What he doesn't know is that she bought a pair for herself, too. Only she doesn't need them for the gym. Instead, she may need them in prison, after the dastardly deeds she has planned."

"Let's hope nobody gets murdered tonight. I'm off duty."

A live band started playing a Hawaiian love song as they approached the Barefoot Beach Café. "Here we are," Karl said. He pointed to the fruity dessert drinks and Pami suggested they share one. They agreed on the *Mangolada*, made from mango, pina colada mix, and pineapple with whipped cream on top.

Karl spread the beach towel on the sand, and they lay down on one elbow, facing each other. Pami dug into the dessert and offered Karl a spoonful of whipped cream. He ate it slowly as he looked into her dark brown eyes. He smiled and offered Pami a spoonful. She licked it slowly, her eyes half-mast with pleasure. Karl smudged a dollop of cream on her lips and went in for a kiss. It was a deep French kiss that placed them into a bubble of obliviousness to the world around them. Karl stroked her long, silky hair as Pami tenderly caressed his neck.

When they finally came up for air, fireworks flashed across the dark skyline and the band was still playing love songs. Pami leaned her head on Karl's shoulder.

A shadow approached them in the dark.

"There you are Karl. I've been looking for you two," said a voice with a distinctive New Zealand accent.

"Oh hey, Neve."

———— ◆◇◆ ————

Jenae had dinner plans that night with her coworkers to celebrate Rhonda's birthday. They all met at the Shore Bird restaurant on Waikiki Beach; which was known for customers cooking their own meat and fish on open air grills. After a quick shower and wardrobe change out of scrubs, she headed over to the restaurant and easily found the birthday table because of the colorful balloons tied to the birthday girl's chair. The smell of barbeque steak made her mouth water. Rhonda wore a white linen sundress that accentuated her innocent 23-year-old figure and around her neck were half a dozen fresh flower leis that were tenderly presented one-by-one as each guest greeted her. It looked like a beautiful, fragrant neck brace.

"Happy Birthday, Rhonda! I'm so excited to celebrate you tonight." Jenae kissed her on the cheek and handed her a bottle of wine in a gift bag that she had just picked up from the liquor store from across the street.

"Thank you, everyone, for coming. You all are my work family and although we're dysfunctional most of the time, I love and appreciate each and every one of you. Now, let's see who can cook the best meat."

The group mingled around the grill zone and shared details about their family lives, which quickly devolved into trauma-bonding stories from work. The camaraderie reminded Jenae of the parallel experiences she had with Pami and Hannah in San Antonio. *Nurses are amazing and fun people. I'm going to miss this when I go to business school.*

As she attempted to flip her steak in flames that jumped up through the grill with a long poker fork, a guy standing in her blind spot handed her a spatula.

"Here, this might make it easier for you."

"Oh, thanks." Jenae turned to grab the utensil. She looked Logan in the eye. "Have I met you before? You look familiar. Do you work at the hospital?"

"No, no, I'm much too squeamish for that. You look familiar, too. Maybe we talked at a bar or restaurant or something."

"Yes, that's it. I remember you from Moose's earlier this week. You were with your dad-friends."

"Right, right. I'm Logan. That was a crazy night, huh? I had to entertain those guys. They were in town for business meetings, and I got stuck with them."

"Oh, bummer. I'm Jenae by the way. You bought my friend and me a drink that night. It's nice to see you again. I think my steak is done now. It looks like all of my friends are back at the table; I'd better get going. Have a good one."

"Enjoy."

Glasses clinked with each toast, chuckles and groans followed bad jokes at the dinner table. For entertainment, the birthday group watched tourists walk down the beach just outside of the patio; lovers held hands after sunset, kids ran in and out of the rising tide, Sand Jesus passed by with two of his disciples, and a recognizable TV actor wandered by with glassy eyes and an unsteady gate. "Hey Tony!" The group yelled in unison, and then laughed when he waved them off with the middle finger and gave them the stink eye.

"Well, this is the best birthday ever. Thank you all for coming. I feel really special," Rhonda said.

As the guests hugged goodbye, Jenae bee-lined it to the women's bathroom before her walk back home. She passed the bar on the way out of the restaurant and saw Logan sitting by himself, finishing a beer.

"Hey, Jenae. How was dinner? It looks like you have a good group of friends."

"Yeah, it was a work birthday dinner. Lots of good people."

"Can I buy you another drink? It looks like your party has broken up."

Jenae felt sorry for Logan sitting by himself at the bar and guilty that she had sent him on his way the other night after buying her a drink. She was safe with the bartender close by.

"I was headed home, but I could have a quick beer with you."

The conversation was light and focused around travel and activities around the island and where they lived.

"I'm at the Kaipuna condo building, not too far from here. Are you familiar with that area?"

"Yes. Coincidentally, I am staying at a place in the big glass building across the street. I know the vicinity very well. I'm surprised I haven't seen you out at the dance club in the neighborhood."

"Ugh, I feel like I'm there every night by proxy. The music beats for the whole neighborhood until late, especially on the weekends. I've been once before with some friends, but I don't like waiting in line to hang out with a bunch of drunken tourists. You know, I can do that at Moose's and listen to live bands instead of boom, boom techno beats. Is that where you go?"

"Being from L.A., I am used to those places. I like the energy and the light shows. Hey, after this beer, can we walk back together? I wouldn't want you to go by yourself after dark."

"I guess so, since we live across the street from each other."

The conversation was awkward on the walk home and as they approached the front glass doors at the Kaipuna. Logan asked a stroppy question.

"Can I come in for a cup of coffee?"

"Funny thing. I don't have any coffee in the apartment because I don't drink it."

"A cup of tea, maybe?"

"Oh, no. I don't think that will work either. I have early plans tomorrow. But thanks for walking me home. Maybe I'll see you around." Jenae didn't offer a hug or her phone number, but waved with a smile instead. Logan's ego was deflated once again, but he wasn't worried because he watched her sleep at night.

Chapter 26

Love is in the Air

The sun beamed, and a cool breeze streamed in through the open sliding glass door in Jenae's bedroom.

"Morning, Jenae, I didn't hear you come in last night. We have a date today, remember? Can you be ready soon?" Pami said.

"What time is it?"

"It's 10 AM. The guys wanted to meet us at the beach at ten thirty or eleven."

"I thought a day date meant starting after noon sometime. I've never been on a morning date before, Pami."

"Well, they're New Zealanders; maybe they have different customs. Or maybe they have plans for tonight."

"I don't know if I want to go. I'm a little concerned that they're such eager beavers; this'll probably be another waste of time. I haven't found anyone that I am really interested in; I'm doomed to settle for a below average guy. I might have to start reading romance novels instead of going on dates." Jenae covered her face with a pillow.

"Oh, come on, Debbie Downer. I'll buy you a chicken fajita pita if you come."

"Well, why didn't you lead with that? Deal. But I still need to wake up and take a shower."

"OK, I can go down and meet them. Just find us at the beach park in front of Fort DeRussy when you're ready."

"Ten-four, good buddy. I will try to be there by eleven."

⸺◆⸺

Karl and Neville body-surfed on morning baby waves as Pami walked up to greet them. Karl stood up in the water and swiftly splashed through the warm ocean toward dry sand, where Pami stood with her hand shading her eyes from the sun.

"So glad you could make it, Pami. You look fresh and beautiful this morning." Karl gave her a side hug, mindful not to get her long blue sarong and white t-shirt wet, even though he could see her bathing suit peeking out from beneath. Pami set her big straw beach bag with sunscreen, tanning oil, and a towel down next to her.

"And you are looking very tan and fit yourself, Karl." Pami had to mentally shake her brain, thinking about his Adonis physique and how lucky she was to have explored every muscle above his waist on their clandestine make-out session the night before. Neville high stepped out of the waves in athletic shorts that doubled as swim trunks as he looked around the beach.

"Hey Neve, how's the water this morning?" Pami said.

He approached the couple.

"Yeah, it's good and refreshing. Where is your friend? Am I the third wheel again today?"

"No, not at all. I promise Jenae will be here soon. She just wasn't ready this early."

The anticipated hurried vertical ride down 16 floors to the lobby turned into a slow-motion dream sequence as soon as Jenae stepped into the elevator and locked eyes with Gad.

"Good morning," Gad said in his sexy Israeli accent.

"Hi, how are you doing?" Jenae ducked her head in a coquettish way while her body tingled.

"Are you going out for a workout? You look fit; like that's something you would do every day."

"I may be dressed for it, but today I'm headed to the beach with friends. I did a triathlon not too long ago. Maybe that's why I'm looking fit."

"Wow, that's cool and very impressive."

"Thanks."

"I have a workout show that I tape at the beach park next door. Maybe you could join us sometime."

"Oh, yeah, I think I have seen you out there before. It looks like fun."

The elevator stopped at five different floors going down, but neither Jenae nor Gad exited. Their eyes were locked, and the sultry energy between the two erogenous strangers became a magnetic bolt. Jenae forgot to hit the ground floor button when she was sucked into Gad's trance. He had a provocative aura starting from his jet-black hair atop his 6'4" frame down his glistening neck to his large defined arms and his perfect athletic legs. She could only imagine what his eight-pack abs looked like underneath his workout shirt. Their eye contact finally broke when the elevator halted with a jolt at the lowest garage level.

When the doors opened, Jenae's face turned bright red the moment she realized that she missed her floor by three levels. Gad forgot to get off on the 5th floor to pick up a friend. They both chuckled and got back on the elevator. Riding up to the ground floor felt like a guilty walk of shame without the satisfaction of a one-night stand. Jenae could have used a few puffs off of a cigarette.

The walk from the Kaipuna to the beach to meet Pami and the Kiwis was a daydream; she recounted her date with Johnny, her awkward walk home with Logan, and the steamy encounter she just had with Gad. Jenae's love and despair over her failed relationship with Tim were long gone in the rearview mirror. Her energy vibrated at a high level, which seemed to attract attention from any man she met. Her body was in dating shape and emotionally she had let go of her insecurities and only focused on activities that brought her joy. She felt like she was finally in love with herself again. That's why she was hesitant about being the wing woman on a blind date. She had never seen this guy Neville, and if he looked anything like his name sounded, it would be a long, painful day. Three tall figures came into view from a distance as they stood ankle deep in the surf. Pami spotted Jenae and waved both arms over her head as if she were signaling a jet to the gate. Jenae approached the group at a slow, steady pace.

"Hi. Sorry I'm late."

"No worries, we've just been goofing around in the ocean this morning," Karl said.

"Have you and Karl met?" Pami asked.

"Not officially, but I saw you at Moose's dancing together. Then you disappeared."

"That was a rough night, yeah." Karl scratched his sunburned forehead.

"Neve, come over here. I want to introduce you to my best friend, Jenae." Pami motioned him with her index finger.

Neve stood up from squatting in the surf. "Yeah, sorry. I was trying to clean out a little scratch I got from the coral reef." Jenae took a step back as if a gust of hunkiness hit her full on when he revealed his chiseled, tanned body. *What is going on? How can there be so many beautiful men in my orbit right now?*

His eyes were piercing and his mouth was inviting when he smiled at Jenae. His face reminded her of the actor Rob Lowe. Neve had that Hollywood look. Jenae's eyes widened as she nodded her head and extended her hand to shake his. Neve gripped her hand with the right amount of strength and maintained eye contact with his million-dollar smile.

"It's nice to meet you," Jenae said.

"It seems like it has taken a while to get time with you. You are a busy lady."

"I didn't know that you wanted to meet me. Work at the hospital does cramp my social life sometimes."

"I saw you the night Pami and Karl met at Moose's. I wanted to come over to say hi, but you were entertaining a table of guys, and I was probably too drunk to make a good impression. I think I was slurring my words a lot."

"Ah, well, we're here now. What do you like to be called, Neve or Neville? I'm confused."

"My friends call me Neve for short. So call me Neve like Steve, yeah."

"Nice to meet you Neve like Steve."

Jenae used her acute listening skills to let every word that Neve spoke with his sophisticated New Zealand accent wash over her. His pronunciation of certain words melted her heart, and his good looks made her entire body quiver.

Chapter 27

Beer and Beaches

The double daters walked to a more populated area on Waikiki where surfboards and yellow plastic kayaks were set up in portable stands to be rented by the hour. They laid out their towels carefully angled for optimal sun exposure. Pami pulled out her bottle of sunscreen and applied it to her face and shoulders before she handed it to Jenae, who followed suit. Karl already had a sunburnt forehead that he covered under a cloth hat with a neck drape. The Americans had never seen such an apparatus called the *Joey*, but Karl assured them that it was a very cool look in New Zealand and Australia. Neve wore light blue exercise shorts that had little structure over his loins, which gave glimpses of his generous endowment.

Karl squeezed out tropical tanning oil on his chest and legs and asked Pami if she could get his back. Pami helped him rub it all over his back and legs as she identified every muscle she polished with unabashed flirtiness. She had earned an A in her nursing anatomy class and had a way of letting Karl know she was at the top of her class without producing a report card.

"And these are your deltoids, and your latissimus dorsi, and trapezius; are you ticklish there? Oh, your hamstrings are so long and tight, it feels like you need a massage to loosen them up."

"Careful there Pami, I don't want the whole beach to see you grabbing my glutes."

"Save that for a later time." Karl said.

Karl and Pami laughed and teased each other on the beach while Neve and Jenae frolicked in the waves. Open water was Jenae's prime milieu for flirting to establish intimacy. She knew all the moves to get the blood flowing and to keep the chase on. It started with a single splash standing in thigh high water, and then she turned away shyly when Neve splashed her back. She laughed out loud and splashed again, but this time with unrelenting blasts with a two-armed assault. Jenae squealed with joy when Neve ran to her, giving her the same car wash treatment. Jenae stayed a few steps ahead and porpoise-dove headfirst underwater to get away. When she surfaced and looked back at Neve, he did the same. Although she could have swam and gotten away with little effort, she waited treading water in neck deep water and smiled when his head popped up right in front of hers.

Neve and Jenae stared into each other's eyes with honest, childlike smiles. A spark of true love ignited. Jenae placed both palms on top of Neve's head and pushed him down while her legs powered under the surface. When he came up sputtering and smiling, she let him gently dunk her in return.

They found the sandy bottom under their feet, and Neve lifted her up while Jenae wrapped her legs around his waist. They fit together perfectly.

"Hey, I think it's afternoon now. Should we go get a beer at Davy Jones Locker?" Sunburned, Karl was ready for a shade break, even with his kangaroo cap on.

"Yeah, sure, let's cool off," Neve said. The foursome found a table in a small, dark, cave-like bar. Through the glass window behind the bartender, kids swam in a hotel pool. Little legs churned, and faces darted toward the underwater window after their skilled dives gave them extra propulsion to the bottom. A young girl passed by the window in her pink bikini and waved as she peeked into the bar.

"I've never heard of this place. This is the coolest bar on the beach. I mean, it's cool and *cool* if you know what I mean. It feels so good," Jenae said.

"We just came upon it on the second day we got here. Neve has bloodhound skills for sniffing out beer."

The quartet was the only group initially in the bar, but as they started their second pitcher of beer, the other ten tables filled up.

"Do you play *quarters* in New Zealand?"

"No, what's that?"

"It's a drinking game and you bounce a quarter off the table and into someone's cup filled with beer. Whoever's cup it lands in has to drink the beer all the way to the bottom and retrieve the quarter with their front teeth. It's a popular game played at university bars," Jenae explained.

"Let's do it. Who's going to get sloshed first?" Pami said.

At the end of the third pitcher of Coors Light beer, all four contestants were equally inebriated and unable to return to the beach. Jenae and Pami happily staggered to the Kiwis' rented condo to continue the date for dinner.

"Neve and I will go out to pick up some food. Is a Hawaiian plate OK with you ladies? There is a restaurant around the corner that's pretty good."

"Sure, can you get some Huli Huli chicken for me if they have it? Jenae, do you have any special requests?" Pami said.

"I like beef or chicken, but I really want some mac salad."

"Sure thing. We'll pick up a few six-packs at the liquor store, too."

The sunburned and red-eyed duo set out on a mission to find food to keep their dates around, at least until the evening hours. The girls lounged on the tropical-patterned couch in the living room of the two-bedroom condo. They took time to assess the likability of the guys from down under.

"So you and Neve seemed to have hit it off. I told you he was cute."

"He is a hunk and so charming. I felt comfortable with him from the get-go."

"Don't you love their accents? Karl is gorgeous, but Neve has a beautiful look. I may have picked the wrong one," Pami laughed.

"Too late now. You found Karl first, and I'm just along for the ride. Have you and Karl talked since the night you met at Moose's?"

"Actually, we had a date at a beach park. I was gone when you came home last night. He called and took me on an early dinner picnic. I think they were hoping you would be around so you and Neve could've joined us."

"That's sweet. I had the birthday dinner for Rhonda last night at the Shore Bird. Oh, and get this, I ended up seeing Logan there. Remember, at Moose's that night, the strait-laced guy came over and bought us drinks before we blew him off? He was with his old dad colleagues."

"Oh no, Jenae. Don't give that guy the time of day. He gives me really bad vibes."

"OK, I'll drop the subject. Back to important stuff...it sounds like you really like Karl."

"I think I do. I've never imagined myself with a New Zealander. I'm not like you Jenae. I like the All-American Man. We'll see how it goes; besides, I need to sample the goods before I decide if I want to put a down payment on a relationship."

"It sounds like it's going to get hot all up in here."

"You and Neve look good together, like brunette Barbie and Ken dolls."

"He really makes my heart go pitter-patter. I know I just met him today, but I like him way more than I liked Tim, and he far surpasses Johnny. Neve makes me laugh a lot too, but he's not funnier than you, Pami. Nobody is."

"Do what makes you happy. We're here to find a couple of premium soon-to-be husbands and we both deserve to be happy."

"Amen, sister."

Chapter 28

Deep Connections

When the men returned with nourishment, they all gathered around a coffee table and ate dinner out of the communal containers filled with chicken, rice, and macaroni salad. Their taste buds were numb, but the warm food felt good in their bellies.

The girls shared stories about their lives in San Antonio, including about their after work hot tub sessions at the unit secretary's backyard, that were usually a big disappointment. Most gatherings turned into the first stage of a pedicure because the ten or so people who showed up would sit on the outer edge of the tub and just soak their feet since the tub was only built for six, maximum. A tiny marijuana joint in a roach clip passed around the tub usually ended up with just two people passing it back and forth because the thought of putting lips on soggy paper that nine others had contaminated was disgusting. A few times, Jenae tried smoking pot, but it made her paranoid and uncomfortable. Any buzz she got from the weak weed was lost when she started worrying that the neighbors would call the cops. She couldn't get past the flashbacks of high school keg party police raids.

"We loved raiding high school parties as new police cadets. Those teenagers got the shite scared out of them when we showed up. Kids scattered like cockroaches when the lights turned on. They had no idea we weren't going to do anything to them. We just had to show up for the neighbor who made the call," Karl said.

"Sometimes, if was a girl's birthday party, we were mistaken for strippers. They wanted to know where our boom box was," Neve said.

"I bet that happened a lot if you two showed up together. You guys are cuter than the cop strippers that showed up to the last party I was at," Jenae said.

"Yeah, show us your boom box!" Pami teased.

Pami and Karl disappeared into a bedroom after the group took Hail Mary selfies in hopes that one or two photos would develop into something recognizable. The key was to hold the camera high and at arms length.

"Keep your pants on Neve, nobody wants to see your tally-wacker," Karl said.

"Maybe you don't, but I want to see what I am working with," Jenae joked.

Playfulness was put on pause when Jenae and Neve stepped out onto the patio to share stories about college. It was the first serious conversation that they had together, and it was authentic because the alcohol had removed their filters.

Neve had started his education in podiatry school but needed more excitement than feet and bunions in his everyday life. Instead, he switched out after two semesters, attended the police academy, and became a cop. Karl was in his cadet class and they became fast friends. Neve had some undercover work assignments on drug cases and enjoyed having a long hairstyle with rock and roll clothing to go with his new persona. Secretly, he wanted to be a rock star, even though he couldn't sing and had mediocre electric guitar playing skills.

Neve was an excellent marksman, and his career ultimately ended the moment he took a fatal shot as the sniper in a hostage situation. He was following orders from the commander on his earpiece, but his soul couldn't reconcile the guilt of ending another man's life that was threatening to kill his own wife. It was unbearable. He relived the shot over and over again. He kept his thoughts and pain inside.

The rifle was steady, and he had the perpetrator's head in his cross-hairs. On his earpiece he heard, "take him out as soon as you have a clear shot." He remembered to breathe out and pull the trigger between heartbeats. Bang. The butt kicked back on his shoulder. The guy was down and dead. "Good job, Neve. You saved a woman's life."

It didn't feel like it to Neve and he was put on leave from the department and spent many months in therapy sessions. Time spent with the department's psychiatrist was helpful to rationalize the shooting, but he couldn't shake the nightmares and sleepless nights. A two-month vacation to America with

Karl was Neve's attempt to try to erase that traumatic memory and replace it with good ones. Alcohol played a big role in Neve's attempt to forget his sins.

Jenae heard the cleaned-up version of his experiences in the police force. He intentionally left out the extent of his inner emotional turmoil that he suffered because of the shooting.

Jenae blinked slowly as she sensed the full impact of his regret, but she still felt compelled to support him. She briefly wondered if their relationship could move forward. His trauma could take some time to unravel and heal.

Jenae was all about saving lives and delivering babies into this world. She tried to lighten the mood and told Neve about her nursing school clinical rotations; her favorite was OBGYN because it almost always had happy outcomes. She loved her midwife professor, who let her actively participate in the delivery process. She told him about never forgetting the feeling of a baby passing through the birth canal as she put pressure on the new mom's sacrum.

Jenae leaned forward, reached around, and put her hand on Neve's lower back as she gazed into his eyes. She explored his beautiful face, which did not give her the slightest suggestion of a pained soul. Neve felt a warmth toward Jenae that he hadn't felt for another woman in a very long time. He wrapped his arms around her shoulders, kissed her on the cheek, and buried his head into her neck. The hug made Jenae's body melt into his as she clasped her hands together around his waist.

They hugged and gently swayed back and forth as if they were slow dancing with only the sound of music in their hearts.

"We could go to my room and get more comfortable. Do you want to have some fun?" Neve said.

"I feel a real connection with you, Neve. I can't believe it came so fast. I would love to have sex with you, but I need to go slow."

"OK, I am happy just spending time with you. I feel the connection too."

Chapter 29

Towel Snaps and Sunset Sails

Inside the condo, Pami and Karl laughed out loud as they chased each other around half-clothed, trying to pop each other's arses with the snap of a twisted-up towel. Pami announced that she was going to take a shower as she turned on the rush of water. Karl happily joined her and lathered her up from behind.

"OK, I think that is our cue to get out of here, Neve."

"Hey, do you want to try to catch a catamaran boat cruise from the beach?"

"Absolutely. I think there are a couple of launch sites by the surfboard rental place. Bye, bye lovebirds! We're going to the beach," Jenae said.

As they walked out onto the sidewalk, Neve grabbed Jenae's hand; she turned and smiled with approval. They held hands all the way to the beach.

At a large hotel on the way to the boats, Jenae took a pit stop in the public bathroom. Neve leaned against the wall as he waited for her return. As he played peek-a-boo with a baby in a stroller nearby, he noticed a familiar face from Moose's hanging around the area. As soon as Jenae exited the ladies' room, Logan greeted her. Neve perked up and watched from a distance.

"Oh, hi, Jenae. It's fancy bumping into you here. I was walking past, and you just appeared like a vision."

"Hi, it's Jason, right?"

"Actually, my name is Logan. I'm your neighbor across the street. I must not have made a good impression on you last night at the Shore Bird."

"Oh, sorry, I'm just a little flustered because we just seem to be at the same place at the same time. Coincidence, I guess. What are you doing here on a weekday afternoon?" Jenae asked.

"I met a client for a late lunch, and I'm checking out the shops here at the hotel. I need to pick up a birthday gift for my sister."

"How thoughtful. OK then, happy shopping. I'm sure I'll see you around again soon." Jenae waited for Logan to walk away and found Neve watching her as she approached. He reached out and pulled her close for a big hug. She felt safe and protected.

"What was that all about? Who's that guy?"

"He's some dude that pops up everywhere I go. This is the third time I have seen him in a week. Weird."

"I saw him with a table of guys at Moose's the night Pami and Karl met," Neve said.

"Exactly. That's when I first met him. He came to our table and bought us drinks.

Then last night he was at the restaurant where I went to the birthday party. He said he lives at the building across the street from mine. He walked me home. I feel like he is tracking me now. But why?"

"Be careful; he may be obsessed with you. You know, a stalker or something. I'll keep an eye out for him while you are with me."

"You're so sweet; that makes me feel safer. Thanks for looking out for me, Neve. Oh, look, a catamaran is coming onto shore. Maybe we can get tickets for the next trip out. It looks a little choppy, but I think we can handle it."

On the boat, Jenae and Neve secured a spot on the coveted trampoline. Neve sat in front of Jenae, leaned back between her legs, and grabbed her ankles for support as the sails billowed out and the boat picked up speed. He absorbed most of the splashes from collisions with the waves, but they both got drenched from below, anyway. They laughed with each spray and hung on to each other as they jostled about. When they reached calmer waters, they sat side-by-side, and each held opposite ends of a beach towel wrapped around their backs.

"So, what are your plans for the rest of your vacation?" Jenae asked.

"I hope I get to see you a few more times before Karl and I go back home. It's going to be really hard to leave now that I've met you." Jenae touched her heart and tilted her head with a smile.

"I've had a really fun time with you, too. Are all New Zealanders like you and Karl?"

"Probably not. You've met the pick of the crop – we are the best the Kiwis can offer. But seriously, what's your schedule like for the next week? Are you available for dinner tomorrow? Neve asked

"Yeah, no not really. I have to work tomorrow all day and then my friend, Mel, from Texas, is coming into town for a week."

Neve's shoulders slumped as he turned his body away from Jenae.

"What kind of friend is Mel? Is he a boyfriend?"

"Oh no, no, no, no. She's a girlfriend, a friend that I worked with at the hospital. Her full name is Melanie, but we call her Mel for short. Although she's kind of butch, so you might be jealous if I were the slightest bit gay; but I'm not, don't worry."

"Whew, that's a relief. So maybe I can call and check in with you, and we can work something out?"

"Sure, I'd like that. I'm sure Mel would like to hang out, too. Although she generally hates everyone I date, so maybe I should keep you two apart for now."

"It sounds like she has a crush on you."

"Don't be ridiculous; we're long-time friends."

Neve walked Jenae home to the Kaipuna as the sun lowered in the sky. It felt natural to ask Neve to come inside with her to hang out at her condo, even though the date had already lasted all day long. Pami hadn't arrived home yet, and they assumed she was passed out with Karl again.

Jenae pulled out a box of crackers and sliced some cheese to go along with the flavored fizzy water she found in the fridge.

"Do you want a snack?"

"Sure. Can I use your phone first? I'm going to try to ring Karl. We had plans tonight, but I'd rather hang out with you, if you don't mind."

"You planned two dates in one day? What a tool."

"Karl asked two girls to meet us for drinks later. They are hairdressers from LA. We don't really know them. Besides, I hadn't met you yet to know that I would choose you over anyone else here."

"Keep the sweet talk coming, and maybe you'll convince me."

Neve picked up the phone receiver and heard a familiar clicking sound. He hung it up and tried again. He heard "tap, tap, tap" again and he hung the phone up for a second time..

"I don't want to interrupt Karl and Pami. I'm sure he'll figure out that I'm not coming."

"Sure thing. Come out on the balcony. Isn't the view stunning looking down toward the beach?"

"It's nice, but to be honest it's hard to keep my eyes off of your beautiful face."

Neve pulled Jenae into his body with one arm around her waist and cupped her face with his hand as he looked into her eyes. Jenae felt her legs go numb and her lady bits tingle. His chest pressed against her breasts as he leaned in for a slow sensual kiss that seemed to stop time. Her head spun a little as he came back in with deep tongue action that probed her mouth in the best way possible. She sucked on his bottom lip and stretched it out as she let go.

As soon as Jenae let Neve's lip go, he caught a glimpse of two men with cameras standing at a window in the building across the street. The windows were less reflective as the sun set, and it was easier to see inside. Neve asked Jenae if they could have their snacks on the balcony. He wanted to calmly observe the two men with cameras pointed in their direction without alarming Jenae.

Neve had a nervous knot in his stomach reminiscent of his sniper days, even though he kept a calm and fun demeanor the rest of the evening. Jenae was giddy with a case of puppy love without a care in the world.

Chapter 30

Mel's Diner

J enae returned home from work via bike. She had time to
pick up a few breakfast items and more crackers and cheese
for her mainland guest on the ride home. When Jenae shopped
for groceries, it brought up a flood of memories about her
relationship with Mel. Although Mel knew Pami and Hannah
well from San Antonio, Jenae was her better friend and main
contact.

She and Mel worked in San Antonio and eventually in
Dallas, too. Mel was tall and lean with a dark mullet hairdo,
fair skin, and freckles. She gave off an Amelia Earhart vibe and
was a serious advocate for her patients. Her washboard abs,
flat chest, and bowed legs gave her power and strength. Their
personalities and physiques were opposites.

*When Jenae moved to Dallas, she rented a two-bedroom
apartment just in case she had visitors, which mostly meant more
room for her little dog, Gremlin. Apartment complexes near
Highland Park were dwellings for trendy young professionals
and a straight shot to downtown on Central Expressway. Shortly*

after she was settled in her apartment, the phone rang on her newly connected landline number.

"Hi Jenae, it's Mel. I was thinking that I should move up to Dallas, too. I've been talking to some recruiters. What do you think?"

"That could be fun," Jenae said as she rubbed her forehead.

"I was thinking that I wanted to branch out from labor and delivery and give adult ICU a shot. Your hospital has an innovative bone marrow transplant unit for cancer patients that I've been looking into."

"You're welcome to stay with me for a few days if you want to drive up and check it out. But you know I'm allergic to cats, so you'll have to find your own place to live if you decide to move here."

"Thanks, I promise it won't be for long. I can't be away from my kitty, Agatha, for more than a weekend."

Jogs after work at midnight on an outdoor path became a healthy obsession for Mel and Jenae that originated in San Antonio and continued in Dallas.

"Let's start with two miles, and then we can build from there," Mel said.

"Go easy girl; Gremlin, and I need to work on our stamina. There's no way I could do this in the heat of the day. I'm glad I quit smoking. You are lucky you never started, Mel."

Evening runs continued to be an after work pastime and stress release in Dallas when Mel moved to an apartment near Jenae. The paths they took around the complexes at night were well lit and level. Pay off at the end of the run was finishing at the swimming pool and jumping in with shorts and a sports bra to cool off. Gremlin barked and hid under chaise lounges while getting splashed by her red-faced mistress.

———◆———

Mel arrived from the airport to the Kaipuna by cab just minutes after Jenae unpacked the groceries. "Aloha, welcome to Hawaii, Mel." Jenae greeted her at the door with a big hug.

"I'm so happy that I get to vacation with you this summer and in Hawaii, no less. This is my first time here."

"Mine too," Jenae said.

"You have an ideal situation; this condo building is gorgeous and right in Waikiki. Thanks for letting me stay with you," Mel said.

"Sure, anytime, but things have changed up a bit since we talked. Hannah's living by herself in my old two-bedroom condo. Pami talked to her and asked if you could stay in my old room while you're here. I hope that's OK."

"I guess so, no problem. I'm thrilled to get a bed, to be honest. So what happened? Why'd you move out?"

"To make a long story short, Hannah slept with the guy I was seeing pretty seriously. She'll probably tell you another story, but that's the basic gist. Anyhow, I'm just staying with Pami here because one of her roommates disappeared. They think she is living with her brother."

"I'm happy as long as I get to explore the island with you and hang out on the beach."

"I can promise you that will happen. And it's good for Hannah that you'll be around this week, too. I don't know if you heard, but her boyfriend, Ronin, was in a terrible car accident while they were broken up. She's very distraught over the circumstances. It was the same time period that Hannah was caught cheating with Tim."

"Wow, that's some bad karma," Mel said.

"Sure is. Ronin is in the ICU at my hospital, in really bad shape. When I visited him a couple of times on my breaks, I just talked to him while he was comatose. I tried to put a good word in for Hannah and him getting back together, but there's no way to know if any of it registered until he wakes up. Anyway, that's the best I can do for Hannah and our relationship. I haven't talked to her since the cheating incident, and I can't seem to get over hating Hannah for her betrayal. I'm not sure I'll ever be able to forgive her."

"It's sad about her boyfriend, but I'm also upset to hear that your friendship is over for now. I'll do my best to check in with her while I'm here," Mel said.

Mel unloaded her bag in Hannah's condo before Jenae took her out for a welcome dinner. She knew they wouldn't be out late because of jet lag and the time change from Texas. They took the obligatory walk down the beach in the pale light reflecting off the ocean waves and sat at a picnic table next to a seafood stand. They ordered skewered spicy shrimp with rice and two light beers. Mel was yawning before she could finish her dinner, and Jenae was pleased to head back to the condo earlier than expected.

"We can get a fresh start tomorrow. I have the day off; let's hang out on the beach and you can get some pigment on that pale skin of yours," Jenae said.

"Yeah, maybe my freckles will all grow together and I can get a proper tan."

"I'll call Walker; he's two-timer Tim's brother. I'll see if he has any time to be our tour guide while you're here. He can probably drive us around the island on some fun excursions. We'll definitely have a good time."

Mel settled in for the night at Hannah's condo. As Jenae headed for the shower, pulling her top over her head, the phone rang.

"Hello?"

"Hi Jenae, it's Neve. I just wanted to check-in on you to make sure you had a good day. Did your friend make it?"

Jenae's heart leapt and her body felt flush.

"Hi Neve. Yes, she did. I just got back from dinner with her. She was wiped out from the long plane ride and she's staying at our other friend's condo while she's here."

"Oh nice. I know this is presumptuous, but I haven't had dinner and I was wondering if you would join me to get a bite to eat tonight?"

"It's so late and I was about to jump in the shower."

"I know, but I just wanted to see you again, and Karl is out and about on his own. To be honest, I'm sloshed, and I need to eat something to sober up."

"Where are you?"

"I could come over to your vicinity and we could eat at the all-night diner by there. Please?"

"Ok, but just because I don't have to work tomorrow and I want a piece of pie with whipped cream on top."

"Great! I will be there in 15-minutes, tops."

Neve waited for Jenae with blood-shot eyes as he leaned against the hostess counter to steady his stance. When she arrived, she instantly thought it would be a waste of her time because his speech was slurred and he was much more intoxicated than he sounded on the phone. She still gave him a hug, and she put her arm around his waist as they found their way to a booth with split red leather seats. Across the table, Neve held Jenae's hand and apologized for his condition. He ordered fried chicken with mashed potatoes and steamed veggies. She ordered a slice of apple pie.

Their dialogue became more coherent after Neve finished his plate of food and gave it time to digest. He became normal again, to the relief of Jenae. Their conversation lasted two hours as they talked about their siblings and parents back home. His parents were divorced, and he had an older brother and a younger sister. He was a middle child like Jenae. They discovered that they had many things in common as they cycled through topics. He told her about his vacation adventures in Los Angeles and San Francisco before their arrival in Hawaii. He and Karl felt at home at Neve's cousin's house in the Bay Area, and Neve was already planning a return visit.

"I feel like I am trapped on a small island living my whole life in New Zealand. I must have been a bird in another life because I dream about flying a lot."

"Maybe you should look into getting a pilot's license. Flying big airplanes around seems a lot safer than flapping your wings."

"That reminds me. My dad used to take me to the fence line at the local airport. He'd check the schedule for arrivals and departures ahead of time and we'd sit in the car listening to the radio and identify the types of planes as they approached the runway. I ate a bag of chips while he smoked his filter-less cigarettes. I think he was trying to escape, too. Hmm... I haven't thought of that memory in a long time."

"It sounds like he planted a seed."

"I bet you could fly a long way in the middle of America. I love the vastness and open space of America. It seems like there are endless opportunities. What's Texas like? Are there cowboys everywhere, like in the movies?"

"We definitely have cowboys, but they drive big pickup trucks instead of riding horses these days. Maybe you can come visit me there when you return to the States."

"I'd love to experience Texas with you. Maybe we could go to a rodeo."

"We have lots of rodeos. I'd love to take you sometime."

"How was your pie? Do you want something else to eat? A midnight snack, perhaps? I think this place is open 24 hours. We could stay until breakfast."

"How about we go back to my place where we can relax? When I first saw you standing at the front of the restaurant, I thought you would pass out on me."

"I'm sorry about that. I hadn't eaten all day and, believe it or not, I didn't drink that much, but it went straight to my brain. Maybe partying so much over the last three weeks had a cumulative effect."

Jenae's apartment was unoccupied because the other girls were working their usual night shifts at the hospital. The walk home had awakened Jenae and Neve, and the juices were flowing by the time they reached the building. The elevator ride up took forever and couldn't keep pace with the rising libido levels surging throughout their bodies. All conversation had been exhausted as they reached Jenae's bedroom and Neve pulled her top up over her head as she released it from catching on her hair. Jenae reciprocated by yanking Neve's shirt off, which revealed his washboard abs and broad chest. Hands were flying over each other's bodies in a fury of passion. Jenae realized where this was going and although she was giving in to her sexual needs, she felt self-conscious.

"I need to take a shower; germs from the hospital are still all over me. Can you hold that thought?"

"I can hold it all night long if you need me to. Do you need me to wash your back?"

"Sure, come on in."

From the FBI surveillance nest across the street, Logan watched through the lens of a camera as Neve and Jenae showcased their intimacy through exposed windows. The other agents had packed up a few days earlier because the mission had expired. The bomb caller had been identified and arrested. He turned out to be the ex-boyfriend of the roommate that Jenae had replaced. His jealousy motivated him to flush his ex-girlfriend and everyone else in the building out during the evacuations to see if she was sleeping with anyone else. The FBI had mistakenly targeted Jenae because she and the girlfriend had almost the exact same physical characteristics.

Logan had offered to stay behind to wrap up the loose ends on the mission, which meant packing up equipment, shutting down the apartment, and removal of the wiretap on the phone in Pami and Jenae's apartment. He'd become obsessed with watching and following Jenae. The jealousy that he felt when she was with someone else had reached an unprofessional and unhealthy level. Logan kept pictures of Jenae in varied levels of undress from her bedroom for his own personal file tucked away in his briefcase.

"Oh shit," Logan said to himself as he saw Neve approach the window of Jenae's bedroom with a towel around his waist and stare straight in Logan's direction as if a spotlight was shining on him. Neve pulled one curtain closed as he dragged the other to meet it in the middle; he dropped the towel to the ground and looked back at Logan. A purposeful slit was left between the curtains, knowing that there was a dirt bag across the way, trying to catch a glimpse.

Chapter 31

Sexcapades

The night of passion left Jenae in a state of satisfaction and relaxation. She was glad the other roommates weren't around to hear the rumblings of their sex escapades; they used every square inch of the king sized bed. Nurses are known for their adventurousness within healthy boundaries, but Neve took her to places she'd never been before. His body was strong and muscular, and he could toss her where he wanted and move her legs into position with ease, like a trained Thai masseuse. She was reliving the mattress gymnastics routine in her head with Neve asleep beside her when she heard the front door open. The roommates were back from work, which meant it was time for Neve to do the walk of shame back to his place.

"Quick, you have to get dressed and get out of here," Jenae whisper shouted.

"Why don't I wait until they go to bed? Are you ashamed of me?"

In truth, Jenae would be proud to show off the gorgeous man she had just spent the night with. She would put him on top of a parade float if she had the opportunity.

"Of course not. I'm just embarrassed a little bit."

"Compared to Pami and Karl's shenanigans, we're like milk toast."

Pami peeked in Jenae's room when she heard talking from that direction.

"Are you up Jenae? Oh, hey Neve. Did you guys have a good night? Looks like that might be the case."

Pami laughed as she noticed articles of clothing strewn across the carpet and a pair of panties hanging from the ceiling fan. "You'd better skedaddle before Mel finds her way over here. You know how she hates your boyfriends, Jenae."

Jenae walked Neve to the elevator in her t-shirt and running shorts; they loosely held hands with just two fingers as they waited for it to arrive on their floor. Right on cue, the doors opened and Mel stepped out.

"Hi Mel, I was wondering when you would get up this morning with the time change and everything."

"I have been up since 3 AM; you know I am an early riser, anyway. I just took a sunrise stroll on the beach. Who's this?"

"This is Neve. He's on holiday from New Zealand. Pami and I have been hanging out with him and his friend Karl lately. Neve and I ran into each other last night after you went to bed. And here we are."

Jenae was awkward as she gave him a quick peck on the cheek and waved goodbye as the doors closed between them.

"I'll call you later, Princess."

"I don't like him, Jenae. You obviously just slept with him. I hope this isn't serious."

<hr />

Neve immediately walked to the building across the road, where he spied a spy spying on him and Jenae. He knew that the cameras were set up on the 17th floor in the fifth apartment on the Mauka side. He had a good suspicion that it was the bloke, Logan, who'd been caught following her earlier in the week. *Was he an elaborate stalker? Why would the cops be watching Jenae? That table of guys at Moose's last week looked like feds. Is she not who I think she is? She seems like a solid girl.*

A delivery person exited as Neve slipped in the front door of the reflective building. He rode the elevator to the 17th floor and got off and waited while residents passed him in the hallway. He noticed a door propped open by a box at the apartment he had targeted. Logan walked out giving instructions to some workers inside. "Finish up packing the equipment and I will be back in a few minutes." When the coast was clear, Neve quietly strode to the doorway and peeked his head inside as he pulled his disposable camera from his backpack. The workers were in the back bedroom cajoling and laying down strips of packing tape on cardboard boxes. As a former cop, he was used to similar situations and Neve had no fear when he took a few steps inside to look around. As he turned his head back to the kitchen area, on the wall, he saw a bulletin board of pictures and dossiers in plain sight, along with a FBI Mission End Order dated a week prior. Neve took a few quick pictures of it and disappeared like a black jaguar in the night.

Chapter 32

Surf Fights and Snapshots

The weather was perfect as usual in Waikiki, and Jenae's beachside activities with Mel went as planned, even though Jenae was exhausted from a night of mattress exercises with Neve. They skipped the shopping tour down Kalakaua Avenue because Mel hated to shop. Instead, they headed straight to a surf lesson booth with discount coupons from the tourist guidebook in hand. Kimo, a short, barrel-shaped man, agreed to take both of them out at the same time. After practicing on the sand by lying down on the surfboards and standing up with knees bent and arms out a couple of times, Kimo said, "OK, that looks good enough. Pick up your boards over your heads and carry them to the water."

The boards were larger and heavier than the girls expected. Jenae was tired before she paddled out to Kimo, standing chest-deep in the surf. Mel was naturally athletic and stood up first, but missed the little wave that Kimo pushed her onto, and she crashed into the worn-down coral reef.

Jenae caught a wave – her first time out, too, but barely got her second foot planted and looked like a crouching tiger more than a graceful dolphin racing the surf. Nobody had mentioned the need for a rash guard, and Jenae quickly discovered why they'd become so popular. Her bare belly and chest began to turn red and burn where her skin rubbed against the surfboard. Chaffing hadn't crossed her mind before the lesson, but she wouldn't forget a protective shirt in the future. Lessons ended with one successful standing ride to shore. Kimo was late for lunch, and the girls were bushed from doing calisthenics on a wobbly board.

The novice surfers found a partially shaded spot and put their towels underneath a palm tree. Jenae offered to walk down the beach to grab a couple of shaved ices from a stand nearby.

"What flavors do you want, Mel?"

"I don't care. Pick something tropical."

At the stand, she recognized Boston Rob.

"Hey, are you guys still here? I thought your group left."

"We did, and we stayed up on the North Shore in a house for part of the week. Johnny is just down the beach. He'll be thrilled to see you again."

"Sure. Send him over. I'm sitting over there with my friend from Dallas. She's visiting this week."

"We're only here for two more nights, and I'm sure he'll want to catch up with you before we go."

As soon as Jenae handed Mel her shaved ice and sat down on her towel, Johnny appeared out of nowhere. He had a big smile and was tanner than the last time she saw him. After introductions, he asked for Jenae's phone number again and assured her that he would try to set something up before he left for the mainland. Mel was not amused.

"How many guys are you stringing along, Jenae?"

"Listen, I deserve a chance to find a good guy after Tim cheated on me with Hannah. How am I supposed to get over a heartbreak like that?"

"You need to give Hannah some grace. Her boyfriend is in the ICU right now."

"Maybe if she'd been with her boyfriend instead of my boyfriend that night, he wouldn't be in the ICU. I'm so pissed off at Hannah. She tried to destroy me, and in the process, she devastated Ronin and his family. His life will never be what was promised."

Jenae's breath was quick and shallow, and her eyes welled up with tears.

"I can't believe you're taking Hannah's side on this. Ronin was or is, I mean – a really good guy, and my heart just breaks for him."

"I'm not on anybody's side. I just want everyone to get along. If it makes you feel any better, Hannah got a call last night from the hospital to tell her that Ronin woke up out of his coma. She went to his bedside as soon as she found out."

"Oh, thank you, Jesus. How's he functioning? Does he remember anything? Can he move his legs?"

"I don't know. I'm sure she'll fill me in when she gets back to the apartment. I do think she knows the errors of her ways, and she really does love him," Mel said.

"Hopefully, Hannah can say sorry to Ronin. I'm not expecting any apologies from her, though. In fact, I won't speak to her again until I get one. Tomorrow, I'll check up on Ronin while I'm at work, and I hope I don't run into her. By the way, I have to work the next two days, but I'll be off at a decent hour, and we can hang out at night. Are you OK navigating the island by yourself for a few days?"

"I checked into some bus tours before I came over. So, I'll take one to Pearl Harbor and maybe to the museum while you are at work."

"Pami might be around during the day to do something, too."

By 2 PM, the girls were back in their rooms for a power nap. After a shower, Jenae lay down on her bed to cool down and quickly passed out. She awoke a few hours later to the phone ringing. It was Walker confirming that he could play tour guide on Jenae's next day off to entertain the nurses. He acted as if sacrificing a whole day to revisit Diamond Head and

Hanauma Bay with the ladies put him out, but cracked up with delight before he could hang up the phone.

"Of course I'll show your friends around the island, if some don't mind riding in the back of the truck and if they're cute."

"I'll get in the back this time, and I assure you they are all too old for you, Jailbait."

"I don't know, Jenae. I have an irresistible smile. They just may look past my youth."

"Thanks Walker, and don't tell Tim 'hi' from me."

"Got it. See you in a couple of days."

Karl and Neve waited in the Walgreens looking at cards while Fox Photo 1-Hr Labs developed their disposable camera film. Karl was curious if the pictures would actually show what Neve thought he saw in the FBI surveillance nest across the street from Jenae and Pami's apartment. Neve's spirit mission earlier in the day gave Karl a little pep in his step and excitement for detective work again. The camera roll from their last week in Hawaii captured images of their beach memories as well.

"You ordered double prints, right, mate?" Karl asked.

"Yeah, you'll get your copies for your photo book. Ok, here we go... the prints are ready."

Outside the store, Neve flipped through the pictures one-by-one and handed Karl the second copy of each.

"A sunset, a flower, you and your Vienna sausage in a navy budgie smuggler, me looking handsome in my pink shark bait t-shirt, that cool cave bar with the cigarette machine, beer, pitchers of beer, me pissing off of a balcony, you and Pami, me and Jenae on the sailboat, another sunset. Aha! Here they are – the pictures from this morning."

"Oh shite, you're right. There are pictures of the girls posted on the walls."

"I told you their phone was tapped. And I swear I saw that piece of crap looking straight into her window last night."

"It says, 'Mission End Orders,' as of six days ago. It looks like they were looking for a bombing suspect and someone in their apartment was involved in it somehow. Yep, it says there that the Kaipuna was targeted with bomb threats, but it doesn't look like they'd seen the real suspects for at least a month and a half."

"According to the orders, they arrested the perps last week. Why are they still following Jenae, then? I'm sure that Logan wanker is operating out of bounds on this assignment. If I see that guy lurking around again, I'll break his arm and there won't be any witnesses. He won't even see me do it."

"Easy now, Neve. You said you saw him loading up the equipment. I bet he's at the airport boarding a flight by now."

"I feel protective of Jenae because she leaves herself vulnerable talking to anyone and everyone. It makes me crazy. I guess it's a Texas thing. This guy could be a serial killer. I'm going to call her just in case."

The phone rang at Jenae's apartment, but there was no answer.

Chapter 33

Boozing and Cruising

Neve couldn't reach Jenae until the next day after her shift. He asked if he could take her out again after work sometime, and she happily accepted for the next night, not taking Mel's feelings or plans into account. She was going out with Mel and a group of girls on a booze cruise that evening, and figured Neve and Karl only had a few more days of vacation before their return to New Zealand.

In between sips of a Blue Hawaiian cocktail mixed with jet fuel, the group of girls danced on the boat bow and took pictures overlooking iconic Waikiki beach. Unlimited drinks were included in the price of the sail, and the ladies took advantage of it.

"This is the worst drink I've ever tasted. I already feel a hangover coming on. By the way, I made plans for tomorrow night with the Kiwis after work," Jenae told Mel.

"What do you mean? You're going out on a date? I came all the way here to visit you, Jenae, and you're going to ditch me for some guy you'll never see again?"

"Don't be so dramatic, Mel. We can make it a group thing. Get Pami and a few of her nurse friends to come. You can invite whomever you want. Not Hannah, though."

"I did meet a few friends today on the bus. I got their numbers just in case you abandoned me. I'm prophetic, I guess."

The atmosphere was chaotic in the condo after work. Jenae had to stay late because another nurse called in sick at the last minute. She had to cover her patients until they found a replacement. When she arrived home at 8 PM, there were seven people waiting to go out. Pami and her friends were sharing photos that they had developed earlier that day. A few guy friends of the nurses showed up, too. "Hey, does anybody recognize this penis? Somebody was taking dick picks with my camera." Pami asked.

Neve called while Jenae was freshening up.

"I'm going to have to meet you at the bar later. Where are we going?"

"They've decided on an old Polynesian place outside of Waikiki, so I think we're all cabbing it, anyway. What's going on?"

"Don't tell Pami, but Karl has latched onto another girl visiting from Phoenix. He canceled on me last minute, but I want to come to where you are, anyway."

"Ok, I won't say anything. I think Pami has someone from Orange County waiting in the wings, so no skin off her back."

"Cool, I'll be there in about an hour. Cheers."

"Can't wait. See you then."

As soon as she hung up the phone, it rang again.

"Did you forget something?"

"Hi Jenae, it's me Johnny – were you expecting someone else?"

"No, sorry. I just hung up with someone."

"My friends and I ran into Mel today and she said we're all going out together. I hope it's all right that I bring a few of my MBA friends along for our final night in Honolulu. We're still meeting at the Polynesian bar at the marina, right?"

"I'm pretty sure that's the one. We'll be leaving soon. See you there, Johnny."

"See you soon."

⚬

Someone called a large taxi van to transport the big rowdy group to the historic bar. Logan stealthily followed behind in a rental car. He had vacated the FBI surveillance post but hadn't yet disabled the tracking device in Jenae's wallet. He had a flight booked out of HNL late that night back to Los Angeles and didn't see the harm in one last attempt to catch her affections. If Logan weren't badged by the FBI, he would have been on their most wanted list for stalking.

The bar was everything they expected. Tucked away in a small marina, the ambiance was true 60s Hawaii. It was a frequent filming locale of the original Hawaii Five-0 television series. Blowfish were preserved and used as lanterns that hung around the bar. Red bulbs backlighting bottles behind the bar maintained the speakeasy's exotic ambiance. Zombie drinks were served in collectable Tiki glasses, and the amount of hard liquor in one Zombie would last an average drinker the entire night.

When Jenae's group walked in, Johnny and his friends were already halfway into their drinks and appetizers of crab cakes and chicken bites.

"Hey! What a great place to end our class vacation! Thanks for inviting us, Mel."

"Sure, Jenae said I could invite whoever I wanted to, and I knew she'd want to see you before you guys left."

Jenae shot Mel a disapproving look as she shook her head. *Mel knows exactly what she's doing, trying to sabotage my relationship with Neve. I just hope he doesn't show up until after these guys are gone.*

"Jenae, don't let me forget to get your contact info in Texas before I go. I'll be traveling to Dallas for meetings this fall and would like to take you out to dinner sometime. I'd love to get some good Mexican food there," Johnny said.

"For sure, I know some really good Tex-Mex restaurants. Are you going to be horse-trading in Dallas? Mel, why don't you give him your number since I don't have a phone in Dallas right now? We can figure it out from there."

Just as Johnny turned to grab a napkin off the bar to write Mel's number down, Neve snuck up from behind, grabbed

Jenae around the waist, and kissed her on the side of her neck. In unison, Johnny and Neve both said, "Who's that guy?"

Jenae's face turned red, and she excused herself to the ladies' room. Mel introduced them to each other and shortly afterward, Johnny returned to the other side of the bar with his friends. He was humiliated, but that wasn't Jenae's fault. Technically, it was Mel's, and Johnny made it seem like his attraction for Jenae went both ways, but it didn't.

Neve blended well with Pami's friends. They reenacted stupid Monty Python skits at the bar and laughed loudly, probably due to the stiff drinks, not sophisticated humor.

Off duty, Logan skirted through the front door and moved to the back of the bar next to some Tiki statues. Neither Jenae nor Neve saw him enter. Logan lifted up on his toes to get a better look over the patrons sitting at the bar. A rush of adrenaline came over him and his heart beat frantically when he saw them together. Thoughts of watching them in intimate moments through a slit in the curtain earlier in the week infuriated Logan. His hands went sweaty, and he accidentally dropped his drink on the tiled floor; the sound of shattering glass made everyone at the bar turn and look.

Both Neve and Jenae caught a glimpse of Logan trying to conceal his face.

"Oh my God, it's him again," Jenae said. Neve felt like his head would explode as his engorged neck veins pulsated. He deepened his voice.

"I'll be back, Jenae. I'm going to get rid of this psycho, for good."

Confident, 6'2", Neve puffed out his chest and stormed to where Logan was trying to hide unnoticed.

"Come on, let's go outside," Neve said with his chin up as he spoke over the top of Logan's head.

"I know what you're up to. I know you are FBI. Why were you watching these girls?"

"Wouldn't you like to know, asshole?"

"I'll tell you what I do know. And that is your mission ended days ago, yet you've been stalking Jenae, anyway. Do you have a problem the department should know about?"

"You don't know anything."

"I have proof of the pictures of the girls that you're holding on to and the stand-down orders you received days ago. If you don't get the hell out of Jenae's life, I'll make an international incident out of it. Or we could keep it personal. Me, I'm a relationship guy. I've made a lot of connections in the boxing ring."

"Alright, alright. Calm down. I'm leaving town tonight and she'll never see me in Hawaii again."

"From one cop to another, you fucked up. You have a big problem; get a new line of work."

Neve watched Logan slam the door of his car before he squealed his tires out of the parking lot. Jenae watched from inside the front door window. She'd never before felt more protected than she did at that moment.

Chapter 34

Playing Hooky

F inding time to spend with Neve on his last day on the island proved tricky for Jenae. She realized that she liked him a whole lot and called in sick to spend one last uninterrupted romantic day with him.

Mel and everyone else thought that she was working a late shift at the hospital.

She loaded up a backpack with essentials for a day of activities and a little black dress with sandals for a special dinner that Neve had promised. She sneakily rode her bike the opposite way of the hospital toward Neve's rental instead. When she knocked on the door, he greeted her with a hot cup of tea, chocolates, and a big, luscious kiss. They sat on the patio and dipped pieces of chocolate in the tea and licked the melted part off with groans of delight. Between bites, they smooched and gazed into one another's eyes. The morning was relaxed and exciting for Jenae, and she felt at home with Neve, but she was nervous that he was leaving. *Am I ever going to see him again? New Zealand is literally on the other side of the world.* Jenae had never been afraid to date men from far-away countries, but they'd always been living in America when they met.

Neve had planned his next trip to the States in his head already. *I wonder if she will visit me in the East Bay when I come back. I'm going to work as hard as possible to put a lot of savings away to make it happen. Living with cousin Nikki will help.*

"I'd like to get to know you better, Jenae. Can we keep in touch when you go back to Dallas? You could send me a postcard with a picture of some long horn cattle or something."

"I suppose so. But you have to write to me first. You can send me a postcard of sheep."

"That reminds me of a joke. Do you know what a Kiwi's first date says to him when she goes to the loo? I'll be right baa...aaaaack."

"Very clever, I get it. He is on a date with a sheep."

The aphrodisiac properties of Ghirardelli chocolate kicked in, and they wandered into Neve's bedroom onto his unmade bed. They were fully clothed and wrapped their legs around each other and kissed between words as they told funny stories. It had a comfortable Sunday morning vibe until the spooning began. Their bodies fit perfectly together and Jenae could feel Neve's knob goblin turn into a hardened beast pressed against her bottom. She smiled and turned over and pinned him to the bed by straddling on top of him and asked, "Is this what you want?"

The morning turned into noontime as they enjoyed a post-coital nap. They grabbed a sandwich on the way to the beach, played in the surf, and dozed on the sand all afternoon. Jenae rode on Neve's back as they body surfed the waves and they lathered each other up with sunscreen to prevent sunburns. She felt butterflies in her stomach every minute of their date.

On the way back to Neve's place, they wandered through an outdoor shopping center that sold souvenirs and semi-precious jewelry. Jenae stopped to try on bracelets and put each one aside, thinking that she would return another day when she had her credit card on her.

"Do you want to stop at this café for a happy hour beer?" Neve asked.

"Sure, this is a cute place that I haven't been to before. I love discovering new places with you."

"Can you order me a light beer when the waitress comes? I need to find a toilet."

The beers had arrived at the table before Neve did.

"Is everything alright?" Jenae asked.

"My life is perfect at this very moment. Thanks for a wonderful day."

"I hope it isn't over. I packed a cute little dress for dinner. Remember, you promised to take me to a nice fish restaurant."

"Of course I do. I'm just trying to hold on to every moment right now. It's going to be really hard for me to get on the plane tomorrow. I'm not ready to leave."

The mood became somber as they finished their beers and walked back to the hotel, holding hands.

Fresh fish prepared by chefs at a fine dining restaurant tasted completely different from what Jenae was used to. The perfectly cooked filet in buttery sauce melted in her mouth. Neve fed her New Zealand green lipped mussels for the first time and she thought she could get used to them. Their final date had turned into an unplanned tantric experience.

———◦———

Karl reappeared late in the evening after a long day with his new love interest from Phoenix. When it came to saying goodbyes, Jenae held back her tears because she knew her heart was breaking.

"I'm going to head back home now. I know you have an early flight and it is getting late."

"Are you going to be ok riding your bike back after dark?"

"It isn't that far and I'll stay on well lit side streets. I should be OK."

"Do me a favor and give me a call when you get back to your apartment, OK?"

"I'll call you." Jenae's voice broke as she looked away with tears in her eyes.

She put her shorts on and hiked her little black dress up to look like a shirt. Neve walked her out and stared down at his empty hands as she unlocked her bike from the railing and adjusted her backpack. They hugged and kissed one last time and their hearts sensed each other's beats as they struggled to let go.

"I'll write to you, I promise."

"And I will write back when I get to Dallas."

She took slow, deep breaths as she slowly rode off into the night. She could hardly stand the pain of saying "goodbye."

Chapter 35

Updates

Pami, Mel, and Hannah were sprawled on the living room furniture when Jenae arrived home from work. She'd just been thinking of Neve and how long his flight took to get to New Zealand. She wondered if he'd showered and gone to bed already. She wasn't angry to see Hannah, but would've preferred that she stayed away.

"We're getting the update on Ronin and his recovery," Mel said.

"How's he doing, Hannah? I heard that he is fully conscious and hasn't lost much memory. Is that right?" Jenae said.

"He's awake, and his brain is doing well, but he's permanently paralyzed from the waist down. My heart is broken for him, but I love him and will stand by him no matter what," Hannah said breathlessly.

"Hannah, you've really stepped up to take care of him. He's in a recovery facility now, right? It seems like you're with him a lot," Pami said.

"It's the least I can do. His family comes in and out of town now that he's stable, so I'm the regular visitor now. I've extended my contract for at least another three months to help him rehab," Hannah said.

"Well, know that he's in my prayers. I can't imagine the stress that all of you are going through right now," Jenae said.

"Thanks."

"I'm sorry to change the subject so abruptly, but we're all invited to an Australian Air Force wine party at the base hangar tomorrow night. Everyone is expected to come because there'll be some really handsome and available Aussie pilots there," Pami announced.

"My social life consists of watching TV at the rehab hospital with Ronin, so I can't go, but thanks for the invitation. In fact, I better get back to my place and give him a call before it gets too late," Hannah said.

Jenae was genuinely sad for Hannah, which is a feeling she never thought would come to her again. She still couldn't stand up and give her a hug, but did sheepishly wave as Hannah departed.

"I don't think I'll have the energy to go all the way across the island tomorrow night after touring around with Mel and Walker all day. I have to work the next morning and I'm exhausted as it is. I can't call in sick again. I'm going to get a bill for my next paycheck if I am not careful," Jenae said.

"That's hilarious. I wonder if anyone has ever gotten a bill for rent and plane tickets for not working enough," Pami said.

"I wouldn't be surprised if I'm the first," Jenae said.

"You'd probably deserve it," Mel said.

"Oh, shut up, Mel. I've juggled my schedule around to entertain you. I arranged for Walker to take us out tomorrow with the other nurses, and I'm doing the best I can."

"Be nice, Mel. Come on Jenae, just one last energy push to go with us. My girlfriends from work are counting on us, and they're planning on driving. Please? Pretty please, with a cherry on top?" Pami asked.

"I'll see how I feel after our day tomorrow, but I anticipate being exhausted, and there's no way that I can miss another day of work before I leave the island in a few weeks. I'm going to bed," Jenae said.

Jenae stopped in the kitchen to grab a snack and a drink, and before she reached her room, Pami jumped up with her arms raised in the air like she was signaling a touchdown.

"Oh wait, I need to tell you something. We had two agents from the FBI stop by today. They just knocked on the door right after I got home from work. They handed me their cards. Look, here they are."

Jenae and Mel inspected the cards as they turned them over back and forth.

"What did they want?" Jenae asked.

"They wanted to tell me that we weren't responsible for our phone bill for the last two months. The government paid for it because they'd been tapping our phone conversations," Pami said.

"What? Why? Holy crap, what's going on?" Mel asked.

"Apparently, they've been watching our condo since someone from this number called in a bomb threat. See that building across the street? They have been watching us through zoom lenses, too," Pami said.

"Is that why we had fire alarms in the middle of the night for two weeks straight? It wasn't for a fire, but a bomb threat? No wonder they were so adamant that we evacuate."

"Apparently, the boyfriend of the nurse who used to live here was arrested for it. They said she had nothing to do with it and left the building without notice because she was so afraid of him. She could've given us a heads up," Pami said.

"So they've been watching us the whole time? Oh my God, I bet they loved the shows they got from my bedroom. I feel totally violated now," Jenae said.

"I guess it'll teach us to keep the curtains closed from now on," Pami said.

"Son of a bitch. I bet that Logan dude who followed me last week was one of the FBI guys," Jenae said.

"I told you he was a creeper. I have a nose for these things. You are too naïve, Jenae," Pami said.

Jenae didn't know what time it was in New Zealand, but she desperately wanted to call Neve and tell him the news. He could make her feel safe again.

Chapter 36

The Australian Air Force wine night was nicer than expected. The hangar was decorated with pictures of wineries from South Australia, and tables held trays of snacks and barrels of ice with nine different types of wine grown in the region. Aussie airmen were eager to take pictures with the traveling nurses, and some made future dinner plans with them for the next few weeks that they would be on the island.

The RAAF crew performed a comedy skit with the backdrop of real military aircraft. Inside jokes went over Jenae's head, but she smiled and clapped, assuming the boom operator depiction had some sort of phallic message. All she could think about was how much sleep she could get by the time the shindig was over and the hour-long drive home that followed.

The ladies and gentlemen, who did not have to wake up for work early the next morning, accepted the challenge of finishing every bottle of Chardonnay, Chablis, and Cabernet. Jenae wanted to have a temper tantrum in the corner, but instead she politely asked for the driver's keys to take a power nap while they finished up having fun at the party. Wine ran out at 2:30 AM, and when the party ended shortly after, the nurses piled into the small hatchback where Jenae slept in the backseat. As the sober one in the bunch, Jenae offered to drive, and luckily she was just awake enough to navigate the deserted highways back to her real bed. She calculated that she could get two more hours of sleep before she had to rise, shine, and bike to work.

"Thanks for showing up at the wine party tonight. I know it's late, but it meant a lot to those guys that we came," Pami said.

"How do we know them again?" Jenae asked.

"One of my workmates has been hanging out with some of them and she really bonded with one guy in particular. They're all good guys. By the way, Marvin was asking where you went. He was the guy you were talking to most of the night."

"Oh yeah, I was telling him about my friend Maribelle, who was from his hometown in Adelaide. She stayed with me for a few months in San Antonio on a nursing excursion from Australia. Maybe he's keen to meet her."

"I think he's keen to meet anyone, but I'm pretty sure he thought he had a chance with you."

"No, no, no. That's not going to happen."

"When we all go out to dinner at Dolly Parton's restaurant later this week, you can tell him that yourself," Pami said.

"Are you kidding me? I'm pretty sure I'm busy that night."

"I didn't tell you what night."

"I'm still busy."

"I don't know what I am doing here with these guys that you keep introducing me to from down under. I can't stop thinking about Neve, but I know it'll never work because we are on opposite sides of the earth. How could there be a more unavailable man in my life?"

"Focus on having fun and not on the outcome. The right thing will happen; don't worry, Jenae. And say a quick prayer just in case." Pami reassured.

———⟨○⟩———

Mel didn't go to the RAAF party that night; she opted to stay behind with Hannah instead. They had conversations about the future and lifelong dreams. Hannah struggled with the thought of spending the rest of her life with a man who had no function below his waist. Her feelings were conflicted because she and Ronin were broken up when the car accident happened, but she wanted to be a good person. Hannah also defended her part in the break-up of Jenae and Tim's relationship.

"I've always thought of Teeim as mine. My mama and Teeim's mama have wanted us to be a couple forever. They both thought that this was the perfect opportunity to realize our fate together. I've always liked Teeim, but it never worked out. I wasn't expecting to meet Ronin on the flight over. I guess I fell hard for him instead. And then, when we hit a rough patch, I fell into Teeim's arms."

"I hope it was worth losing a good friend over. Have you talked about it with Jenae?"

"She wouldn't give me the time of day. She hates me."

"Maybe you could approach her starting with an apology."

"For what? She should have known that Teeim and I had this thing brewing underneath. She shouldn't have gotten with him in the first place."

"I'm sure she sees it differently. What's the status between you and Tim now?"

"We don't talk much. I think Walker is upset with me, too," Hannah said.

"From what I've seen, Walker and Jenae are really close. She treats him like a little brother, and he takes care of her, too. He was really nice to take us out to the beaches today. We had a fabulous time. Honestly, I don't know how Jenae juggles everything in her life. I swear she doesn't sleep. Do you think she takes drugs to keep awake, like amphetamines or cocaine?" Mel said.

"I doubt it. She really is a prude when it comes to that stuff. Besides, she's a nurse; why would she risk her license?" Hannah said.

"She told me once that she takes vitamin C for breakfast every morning," Mel said.

"Yeah, so what?"

"I think she meant cocaine. You know, vitamin C is slang for cocaine."

"You're hilarious. Have you seen her bedside table? She literally has a huge bottle of chewable vitamin C on it. She got two bottles the first week she came. Do not start that rumor, Mel." Hannah said.

"I'm really irritated at her now. I guess my mind could spin it around on her."

"Why are you mad at her?"

"I just feel like I came out to see her, but she's so busy with this guy and that guy, and I'm just an appendage or an afterthought in her plans," Mel said.

"I thought you came out to see all of us. What am I? Chopped liver? I mean, I can't believe that I am defending her, but she has done a decent job of including you while you've been here."

"I know. I guess I just wanted more."

"Like what? Do you have romantic feelings for her? You sound jealous. Sorry to tell you this, but I'm positive that she is strictly dickly."

Hannah laughed out loud, and Mel's face turned red.

Chapter 37

Skinny Dipping

M el took off. She booked an earlier flight home the night after the Aussie wine party and took a cab to the airport without ever saying goodbye. For Jenae, it felt like a gut punch, but it also took a lot of weight off of her shoulders.

A picture postcard of bodysurfers on Waikiki sat on the dining table and caught Jenae's eye as she vacuumed the living room. *Huh, I wonder, is that for me? Oh, it is for me. Aw, Neve must have posted it before he left.* She held her heart as she read it out loud to herself, "Thinking of you every minute that I am flying over the Pacific Ocean back to New Zealand. I can't wait to body surf with you again. Here is my address and phone number if you miss me too much. XOXOXO, Neve"

Jenae immediately started counting on her fingers, trying to figure out the time change from Hawaii to New Zealand. She remembered Neve telling her that they were ahead but behind, but it was the next day. She was confused. Nevertheless, she wanted to fill him in on the FBI surveillance operation, the bomb threats, and Logan's likely involvement.

Jenae put the postcard under her pillow for privacy even though she knew Pami had already read it when she brought it up from the mailbox. She needed to focus on her next set of guests. Manny was a childhood friend who was traveling with his law school buddy on their Bar Trip. They had just taken the BAR exam after graduating from law school, and it was a tradition to take a big trip before their lives were consumed by work at a law firm. They had been to Australia, New Zealand, Samoa, and Hawaii was their last stop.

Manny was two years older than her, but Jenae had crushes on him from age fifteen. All through high school, she imagined what it would be like to go out on a date with Manny. He was handsome, kind, smart and best friends with the boys of the family that lived across the street. She could have fallen deeply in love with him if the conditions were right. In fact, she was sure she'd fallen in and out of puppy love at least three times. Throughout Jenae's childhood, kids from the neighborhood of all ages played baseball, kickball, and nighttime tag together; Manny was often part of the posse, even though he lived in a different area. Manny was always up for a good time, and Jenae planned to show him that good time in Hawaii, with Pami as her reliable wing-woman. She could finally go on her infatuation dream date. It would've been easier had Neve not occupied her mind at all times, but Manny was a perfect match for her on paper.

With just two weeks left on her contract at the hospital, Jenae called the travel agency to book her plane ticket home;

the end in sight crystallized. She felt a visceral letdown in her gut. The reality of starting a master's program and working twelve-hour weekend shifts would be the exact opposite of the lifestyle that she lived for the last three months. Jenae was grateful for most of her experiences in Hawaii, but she was ready for the challenges ahead.

———◆———

Manny and Pete were enthusiastic when they arrived at Jenae's front door. They both greeted her with a big hug.

"Hi Jenae. You look great; thanks for letting Pete and I crash here for a few days on our final leg. We're so lucky that you're living here," Manny said.

"It's good to see you too. It's been a long time, nice to meet you, Pete. Welcome! I'm not here for much longer; you caught me just at the right time. Are you jet-lagged, or are you ready to go out tonight?" Jenae nervously blurted.

"We're ready and willing. We've been saving the best for last," Pete said.

"My roommate, Pami, is going to join us if that is OK."

The foursome walked the streets of Waikiki, pointing out historic sites and watching Hawaiian Hula performances at the large shopping center. By happy hour, they predictably found a table at Moose's and ordered the first round of Long Island Iced Teas.

"Cheers to finishing law school and passing the BAR," Jenae said.

They clinked their glasses together and quickly finished their first drink as Manny and Pete told the girls stories about their travels to the southern hemisphere. Jenae was especially interested in finding out what New Zealand was like.

"New Zealand was cool. We hiked around the South Island on glaciers and stuff. The roads are mainly two lanes, and they drive on the other side of the road, so that was tricky. Oh, and there really are a lot of sheep in the countryside – and birds. We got a big one stuck in the grill of our rental car. Poor bastard," Pete said.

"OK, the next round is on me." Manny ordered the drinks at the bar on his way to the restroom. He pressed the glasses together and carried all four in his hands as he walked carefully, trying not to spill a drop.

"Let's all buy a round and see who is still standing when they are all gone. The next round has to be consumed while holding a handstand. I call it because I'm buying," Pete said.

By the third round, Pami's head was spinning, Jenae laughed hysterically at not-so-funny jokes, and Manny and Pete did handstands drinking out of straws from their glasses placed on the floor. Manny held Pete's legs up and then Pete held Manny's legs while he sip-chugged the entire drink upside down. Jenae bought the last round but couldn't bring herself to drink it.

"Here Manny, this one is yours, too. This was your idea. You can handle an extra drink, right?" Manny manned up and swigged his fifth Long Island Iced Tea and quickly became the most inebriated of the group. If they hadn't left the bar on their own, they would've been bounced out for being over served.

The sun was starting to set, and the foursome headed for the beach, hoping to catch the green flash that everyone talked about. By the time they staggered to the sand in front of a hotel, the sun had already gone down and darkness had set in.

"Ah, crap. We missed it." Manny slurred.

"Let's go skinny dipping instead," Pami smiled as she pulled down her shorts and walked to the waterline in her underwear. She discarded her shirt before diving into the surf and turned around to make sure the others would follow. She swung her soggy panties around like a Steelers' Terrible Towel and lead them out to sea.

"Great idea. Let's do it," Pete said.

The quartet delighted in their own drunken world as they swam in the surf and did dolphin jumps and side splashes, imitating their favorite marine animals. When they looked toward shore, they noticed flashes of light from the beach. Tourists were snapping pictures of the lunatics' naked bodies as they screamed and laughed with joy. They would've been embarrassed had there been a sober cell left in their bodies.

Pami decided that she was ready to get out and went to retrieve her clothes that she had placed on the cement levy wall.

Instead, she found pieces of clothing floating in the surf as the tide rolled out.

As she collected all the clothing that she could find, she panicked a little, but had just enough garments for Pami and Jenae to have an outfit each. They scrambled to shore after putting the odd shirt and shorts on, which were mostly the guys' clothes. Without guilt or sobriety, Jenae yelled at the guys still in the surf, "We're cold. We'll meet you guys back at the condo!"

Pami found her wallet in the sand and called a cab. When Jenae and Pami opened the door to the taxi, the cabbie refused them service because of their wet exterior. Instead, they walked down the main road as if nothing was wrong. They could have been mistaken for perfectly normal tourists, except they were completely soaked and had mascara dripping down their cheeks. As they giggled along, a small group of men caught up to them. It was Sand Jesus and his disciples.

"Hey, Sand Jesus. Where do you live? We always see you out, but nobody gets to talk to you," Pami said with a drunken twang. Sand Jesus did not reply.

As they walked along at the same pace, Sand Jesus looked at Jenae and said, "Do you want to get a beer with me sometime?" Pami howled in laughter and Jenae felt flattered beyond belief.

Together, the newbie lawyers put their reasoning skills into action even under drunken duress, hypothermia, and public humiliation. They found deflated water floats lying on the beach that they wrapped around their waists as cover-ups. They picked up Pami's shirt too, which fit Pete with the buttons undone. Manny remembered the path that they walked to get there and an hour later, the girls heard a knock on the door.

"What took you so long?" Pami said.

"You stole all of our clothes." Manny told the story of their walking journey through Waikiki with just shoes on their feet and plastic pool toys around their privates.

"People laughed and pointed at us the whole way back because we were wet, and essentially naked, with plastic wrapped around our bodies. So, after walking about a mile walk, we come up on the dance club across the street; that's how I knew we were at the right building. The line of people outside were really laughing and pointing at me in particular. I just chuckled along – until I looked down and realized that the pool lounger's clear viewing window was right over my crotch. I had given a peep show to everyone I passed on the sidewalk. How embarrassing." Manny chuckled as he adjusted his pool-float sarong.

The girls laughed and luckily the guys weren't the least bit mad about being abandoned with no clothes. Manny slept in the same bed as Jenae, but their attempt at a hot night of passion was a complete failure. Excessive alcohol dampened their libidos, and the timing was way off; her schoolgirl crush for Manny was overshadowed by her feelings for Neve. She couldn't get Neve off of her mind.

Chapter 38

Making Amends

A call from Tim caught Jenae off guard as her final week in Hawaii approached.

"Hi, Jenae. I know we haven't spoken much since the triathlon. I heard that you've been seeing somebody."

"Yeah, I guess I have found a guy that I like. What's up, Tim?"

"Walker said that you're leaving next week and we're getting a group together to go waterskiing at the bay by the Marine base, it's the same bay we swam for the triathlon. A few of us have rented a boat on Saturday. I remember you told me that you liked to waterski."

"Yeah, we went to the lake every summer as a kid. My uncle had a boat that we ran every minute of daylight."

"Do you want to come with us? I want to warn you that Hannah is coming, too. We're just friends again; nothing weird. Can we just finish out this summer with a good memory between the three of us?"

"I suppose that would be the right thing to do. I don't know though; it's going to be awkward and uncomfortable."

"It would mean a lot to me if you came. I promise to make it fun. Please come."

"Ok, I'll come. Thanks for inviting me."

Tim's call reminded Jenae that she should check in with Neve, now that he'd been back home for a few days. She dialed an endless string of numbers, starting with her calling card, and finishing with Neve's international number. The ring tone startled Jenae because it was low pitched, more like a grinding static sound than a ring. Her stomach was filled with butterflies. *Urt, urt...urt, urt...urt, urt...urt*. No answer. She dropped the phone receiver on its stand like it was a hot coal. She would try again later in hopes that her nerves would settle down by then.

Cruising on the boat with Hannah and Tim became less uncomfortable, but never enjoyable, for Jenae as the afternoon progressed. She talked to the other guys on the boat to avoid self-conscious moments of insecurity. Tim showed off his slalom skills on one ski by cutting across the wake and catching air before splashing down again. Jenae drove the boat when he skied and did her best to make him wipeout by weaving back and forth and circling back around to choppy waters. When it was her turn to ski, Jenae showed her best effort by placing the rope handle between her legs and elegantly stretching her arms straight out from her sides. Hannah barely skied one time and kept to herself. It was apparent to everyone that the aftermath of Ronin's accident weighed heavily on her. She wasn't a happy, flirty girl anymore.

On the drive home, Tim asked Jenae if he could take her to the airport for her departing flight. Jenae was surprised, but gratefully accepted his offer.

———————⋯⋯◇⋯⋯———————

Jenae rode her bike to work for the last time, and the bus passed her on the narrow road, giving her ample space. The bus driver smiled and waved, and she waved back. They'd been road buddies for the last three months after the driver realized she wasn't going anywhere.

When she arrived at her unit at the hospital, the break room was set up with streamers and a banner that said, "Mahalo, Jenae. We will miss you." Jenae's heart melted as Rhonda gave her a hug and put a fresh-flower lei on her shoulders. The other nurses gathered around with smiles and good wishes. Jenae gently lifted the Hawaiian necklace from one side to smell the sweet fragrance of the tropical flowers that surrounded her head. The nurse manager made an impromptu speech as everyone gathered around, holding colorful paper plates filled with banana-nut bread and fruit. "I wasn't sure how this assignment was going to work out with you, Jenae. It was rocky at the start, but once you got acclimated, you stepped it up and became a vital part of our staff. Thank you for coming all the way to Hawaii to help us out. We truly are sad to see you go. If you want to stay longer, I have an extended contract for you in the office." All the nurses laughed, including Jenae. She thanked them for putting up with her and for being her friends. Her heart was full.

Tim came to pick Jenae up and help take her bags to the truck, where he did all the heavy lifting. It was just Tim and Jenae; Walker had said his goodbyes earlier that day.

"So, where do you want to go for dinner?"

"You don't have to take me out to eat."

"I want to treat you to a nice meal before you get on the plane. We have plenty of time before your flight leaves. Is Mexican OK?"

"OK, sure, that's very kind of you, Tim."

They drove in the direction of the airport and parked at a big Mexican restaurant on the way.

"I'll have a margarita on the rocks with no salt, please."

"And for the gentleman?" the server asked.

"I'll try your local beer on tap, please. Thanks."

They shared a basket of tortilla chips and salsa. Tim mixed the hot and the mild sauces together to get the spice level just right. When the drinks arrived at the table, Tim raised his glass to make a toast.

"To one hell of a summer. You hold a special place in my heart, and I hope we'll always stay in touch." Jenae clinked her big margarita glass to his beer and looked directly in his eyes. "Here, here."

"I guess time can heal wounds," Jenae added.

"We could talk about the bad stuff that happened, but I'd like to focus on moving forward," Tim said.

"You're right. I don't want to talk about it. You broke my heart, and that's it."

Tim looked down and then away toward the door. The waiter interrupted their conversation with precision timing to take their food order.

After dinner, Tim held the passenger door open for Jenae and offered her a hand up into the cab of the truck. "Thank you, and thanks for dinner, too."

"See, dinner wasn't so bad, was it?" Tim said.

"I guess not, but I don't know when I'll see you again," Jenae said.

"It may be sooner than you think. I'm at a point where I can separate from the military, and I might just go out into the civilian world next year."

"You have my number, so let me know if you come to Dallas."

"I will. I'm sure I'll be in the Houston area for a while because of Mama."

The red truck pulled up along the curbside in approximately the same spot that had picked her up with Hannah three months earlier. Tim unloaded her suitcases and a boxed twelve-speed bicycle onto a cart for her.

"OK, I guess this is it." Jenae straightened out her shorts and gave Tim a side hug.

"I'm going to miss you, Jenae."

"I know. Give me a kiss, Tim." Jenae tapped her finger on the side of her face. Tim leaned in for a smooch, and Jenae did not turn her head for a kiss on the lips. He quickly gave her a peck on her cheek and said goodbye.

<hr/>

The flight to Los Angeles was delayed by an hour, which gave Jenae a chance to call Neve again from the pay phone at the airport. She felt more confident dialing and was ready for the low buzzing ringtone. *Urt, urt...urt, urt.*

"Hello." Jenae's heart fell to her stomach.

"Hi Neve, it's Jenae calling from Honolulu." Neve sat down because his knees went weak.

"I've missed you, Jenae. I'm so glad you called."

"How was your flight home? Are you getting back into the swing of things at work?"

"Yep, yep. I'm back into my monotonous schedule. I am so glad that you called me. I left something for you in your backpack. Did you find it?"

"No, but I got your postcard."

"Perfect. Well, I want you to read the card once you're airborne. It's in one of the pockets."

"Aw, how sweet.

"I hope you like what I wrote... and feel the same way that I do." Jenae's heart skipped a beat.

"Hey Neve, before we hang up, I wanted to tell you about some federal agents who came to our door after you left. They'd been watching our apartment for the whole time I lived there. There were some bomb threats earlier in the summer and it turns out the boyfriend of Pami's previous roommate made them."

"I know."

"What? You knew? How? Why didn't you tell me?"

"I figured it out, and I didn't want you to be scared."

"Why wouldn't you tell me? Now I'm mad."

"I would have said something if I thought you were in danger. But I knew you were OK by the time I left. I barely figured it out a day or two earlier. Don't be angry with me, Jenae. Be mad at the psycho-stalker, Logan, who followed you around after the operation was over."

"I knew he was part of something weird."

"Remember? I had a not so friendly conversation with him at the Polynesian bar before I left. He shouldn't be bothering you anymore. He's long gone from the islands," Neve said.

"Well, OK, but I'm still a little mad that you didn't warn me."

"I hope you can forgive me, Jenae. I wish I could kiss you right now."

Jenae's defensiveness dropped to the floor.

"I wish you could kiss me, too."

"Have a good flight and send me a postcard from Texas. It'll be much cheaper than this phone call. And don't forget to open my letter when you take off."

"How could I forget? Bye-bye."

"Cheers, talk to you soon."

Chapter 39

Aloha

The customer service agent dressed in a blue and white Hawaiian shirt started boarding passengers as Jenae ended her phone call. She was in the fourth group to board and still had time to sit down in the open-air gate area before she was allowed to line up to get on the plane. She took one last look around at the tropical flowers growing along the walkway and listened to the soft background music of ukuleles on the overhead speakers. Her eyes closed as she took in a big breath, trying to commit Hawaiian fragrances to her memory.

She settled into her window seat toward the back of the plane and was pleased to see the middle seat next to her was unoccupied. She wasn't in the mood to talk to strangers and was hoping to sleep a few hours on the red eye flight back. Twinkling lights of Honolulu disappeared into the night as the plane swiftly left the island's airspace. Mainland was only five hours away, but for the last three months, it felt like it could have been as far away as the moon. She came to understand the meaning of "island fever." Jenae's time in Hawaii flew by at a snail's pace.

She thought back on her experiences in Hawaii as the plane headed eastward.

I had so many adventures and by far the hardest was riding an emotional rollercoaster. My friendship with Hannah just died when she betrayed me. I can't get over it and act like I trust her again. It's dead and gone and can stay at the bottom of the Pacific Ocean as far as I'm concerned. Mel destroyed our friendship, too. I mean, she just took off and didn't even say goodbye or thanks or anything.

Pami, on the other hand, was a true-blue friend through and through. She cracks me up with her antics and always makes me feel good about myself. She's the best.

The triathlon was epic, even though I thought I would die of heatstroke. I'm going to hang on to that t-shirt forever. I can't believe a car hit me on my bike; I was more pissed off than hurt. Thank you, Jesus, for keeping me intact. But Tim really broke my heart. I thought we could have had a future together. It seems like he would like to try again, but I'm not that kind of girl who gets over cheating just like that. I could never trust him again. I suppose it was better to find that out early. Love only hurts when your heart gets broken. I would like to keep up with Walker, though; he's a great friend.

Exploring the other islands with Niles and then Mom was really special, too. It seems like Niles has worked through his marital issues. I can't believe how daring mom is. She would pretty much do anything if you double dared her. How did she jump off that rock on the North Shore and not break a hip? I was scared to do it, but with all of those youngsters watching me, I couldn't let her show me up. And it was nice of her to take care of Gremlin while I was here. Wait a minute; who took care of Gremlin while Mom was here with me?

Working at the hospital was definitely a challenge because it was part of the bigger experience. Working on vacation or vacationing while working probably should be avoided in the future. I really thought I was going to be fired a few times, but I pulled it out in the end. My workmates were still really good people.

I suppose I kind of like Johnny because he's marriage material, but I kind of don't because he isn't my type. He'd be perfect if we had an ounce of chemistry together. I wonder if he'll try to call me in Dallas. And then, the Manny situation threw me for a loop. How many years have I pined after that guy, and the romance was nothing more than a fizzled-out firework?

Maybe that was because I'd already fallen in love with Neve. What? Did I really think that? I'm pretty sure that I am in love with Neve from New Zealand. Oh, he's just so handsome, and has a dreamy accent, and holy moly, our physical attraction is out of control. He's so attentive, and he thinks about me. But he's so far away.

I forgot! He said he left me something in my pack.

Jenae waited impatiently until the seatbelt sign turned off and she excused herself out of her seat to retrieve her backpack stored in the overhead bin above her row. She checked through the bag once she returned to her seat and buckled up. Inside was a plain brown gift bag with a small gift wrapped in white tissue paper. She opened the gift first. It was a charm bracelet with a silver heart between two silver dolphin figurines.

Oh, I love it. He is so romantic.

She opened a card that she found inside a pocket of her backpack, and read the message to herself.

My dear Jenae, I've had the best two weeks of my life in Hawaii, mostly because of you. I'm under a spell and can't stop thinking about you. You have captured my heart, and I promise that I will come back to the States to love you even more. I have fallen for you, Jenae. Love, Neve XOXOXO

Jenae couldn't speak or even think. She put on the bracelet and spun each dolphin around, thinking of her memories with Neve.

I can't believe he loves me. I never thought this would happen. I never thought someone that I loved could fall in love with me; nothing else matters. How did I get so lucky?

Jenae's heart was bursting, and her eyes filled with tears of joy that slowly rolled down her cheeks as she dreamed about her future with Neve.

The End

BIG ROCK

Acknowledgements

First thanks go to my unwavering cheer team and first readers – My daughters A and S. They may have endured a little discomfort while reading the saucy parts of my story, but they were always gracious with their feedback.

A big thank you to my ride or die girlfriends, DM and JJ. DM always had an angle and JJ is an angel.

Thanks to my super talented sister who encouraged my writing from word one and every step along the way.

Thanks to all of the fabulous nurses who make lives better, and to every writer who shared their expertise with me (including All Write Well and The Assist) to make this book possible.

Most of all, thanks to my husband, who has supported all of my passions for three decades.

And... a huge thank you to readers who bought Big Rock and stuck with it until the end. I appreciate your feedback and if you have time to review it on Amazon and click on some stars, it will help others find this story too. Mahalo.

— Big Bay — Coming soon in summer of 2024 . Jenae's adventure in love continues on the mainland with budding love and suspense in the shadow of the Golden Gate.

— Big Kiwi — Coming soon in fall of 2024 . Follow Jenae to New Zealand for more adventure and love.

To read more of Reggie's books, or nominate your favorite nursing student for a scholarship, or link to a review page, click on the QR code or link below.

https://linktr.ee/reggiebrick

Big Rock Characters

<u>Jenae</u> – Twenty-six-year-old traveling nurse. She worked in San Antonio and Dallas in big medical centers in adult and newborn baby care. She is spending three months with her two friends in Honolulu during the summer of 1988. She is tall, brunette and fit. She exercises everyday.

<u>Hannah</u> – Nurse from San Antonio and part of the traveling nurse trio. She is petite, blonde with a bubbly personality and a sunshine smile. She works in NICU and grew up in Houston. She organized the traveling nurse trip and rooms with Jenae in Honolulu.

<u>Pami</u> – The third nurse in the three-amigo Hawaii group. A PICU nurse from the northern midwest originally. She is a funny and true friend. She does not cause drama nor does she exercise.

<u>Mel</u> – Entitled serious nurse friend from San Antonio and Dallas.

<u>Tim</u> (Teeim) – A 27 year old marine based in Kaneohe, HI. from south Texas. He grew up with Hannah and played football at the Naval Academy. He is fit and muscular and has a thick neck and skinny legs.

<u>Big Red Truck</u> – Tim's main vehicle

<u>Blue 12 Speed Road Bike</u> – Jenae's main vehicle

<u>Ronin</u> – Hannah's Hawaiian boyfriend

<u>Rhonda</u> – Jenae's fair skinned Hawaiian friend from work

<u>Uncle Dingle</u> – Tim's Uncle from Texas

<u>Niles</u> – Jenae's older brother

<u>Sand Jesus</u> – Local icon of Waikiki

<u>Walker</u> – Tim's teen-aged brother

<u>Mom</u> – Jenae's mother who is a nursing professor and breastfeeding expert

<u>Dad</u> – Jenae's father who is a medical doctor

<u>Logan</u> – FBI agent

<u>Johnny</u> – Recent MBA grad from Boston

<u>Boston Bob</u> – Johnny's friend

<u>Karl</u> – New Zealander and ex-cop on vacation with his buddy, Neve.

<u>Neve</u> – New Zealander and ex-cop on vacation with his buddy, Karl.

<u>Manny</u> – Childhood friend of Jenae

<u>Pete</u> – Manny's law school and travel buddy.

Made in the USA
Columbia, SC
07 February 2025

52750448R00193